WAYNE STINNETT

FALLEN OUT

A JESSE MCDERMITT NOVEL

Caribbean Adventure Series

Volume 1

DOWN ISLAND PRESS

2014

Published by DOWN ISLAND PRESS, 2014
Travelers Rest, SC

Library of Congress cataloging-in-publication Data
Stinnett, Wayne/Wayne Stinnett p. cm. - (A Jesse McDermitt
novel)

ISBN-13: 978-0692225073 (Down Island Press)
ISBN-10: 0692225072

Most of the locations herein are also fictional, or are used
fictitiously. However, I took great pains to depict the location
and description of the many well-known islands, locales,
beaches, reefs, bars, and restaurants in the Keys, to the best of
my ability. The *Rusty Anchor* is not a real place, but if I were to
open a bar in the Florida Keys, it would probably be a lot like
depicted here. I've tried my best to convey the island attitude in
this work.

FOREWORD

I'd like to thank the many people who encouraged me to write this fourth novel, a prequel to the first three, especially my wife, Greta. Her love, encouragement, motivation, support, dreams for the future, and the many ideas she keeps coming up with have been a blessing. At times, I swear she was a Key West Wrecker in another life. Or maybe a Galley Wench, I'm not always sure. A special thanks to my youngest daughter, Jordy, for her many contributions and sometimes truly outlandish ideas. While only a twelve year old mind can conceive of some of the wacky ideas she has, many of them planted a seed in my mind that found their way into the story. I need to thank our other kids, Nicolette, Laura, and Richard for their support and encouragement.

I also owe a special thanks to my old friend, Tim Ebaugh, of Tim Ebaugh Photography and Design, for the cover work. You can see more of his work at www.timebaughdesigns.com.

Lastly, where would any writer be without great proof readers? While I can come up with a decent story line and characters, it's Karen Armstrong and her mighty red pen and Donna Rich, with her computer wizardry that put the polishing touches on it all. Thanks also to Beta Readers Thomas Crisp, Marcus Lowe, Timothy Artus, Joe Lipshetz, Nicole Godsey, Debbie Kocol, Mike Ramsey, Alan Fader, and Bill Cooksey.

If you'd like to receive my monthly newsletter for specials, book recommendations, and updates on coming books, please sign up on my website:

www.waynestinnett.com

Jesse McDermitt Series
Fallen Out
Fallen Palm
Fallen Hunter
Fallen Pride
Fallen Mangrove
Fallen King
Fallen Honor
Fallen Tide (November, 2015)

Charity Styles Series
Merciless Charity
Ruthless Charity (Winter, 2016)
Heartless Charity (Fall, 2016)

The Gaspar's Revenge Ship's Store is now open. There you can purchase all kinds of swag related to my books.
WWW.GASPARS-REVENGE.COM

DEDICATION

To my loyal readers.

Many of you have emailed me, wanting to know more about Jesse, Rusty, Julie, Jimmy, the other islanders, and their backstories. This prequel to the series should shed more light on how Jesse came to live in the Florida Keys and hopefully show a side of these characters you couldn't see in the series.

"The world was all tied together in some mysterious tangle of invisible web, single strands that reach impossible distances, glimpsed but rarely when the light caught them just right."

Travis McGee
The Green Ripper, 1979

MAPS

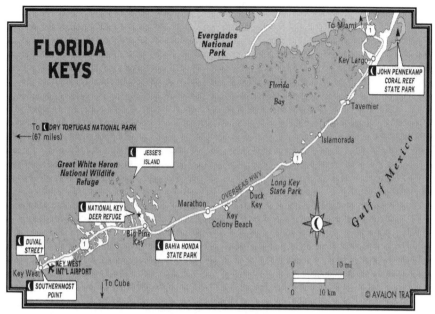

The Florida Keys

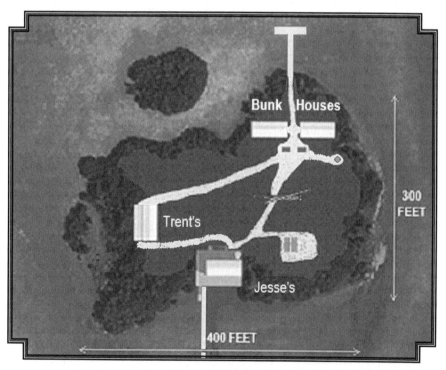

Jesse's Island

 PROLOGUE

Rising from my bed in the Bachelor Enlisted Quarters, I stretched and thought, *Today's the day. My last day in the Marine Corps.*

It was twenty years ago today, that the door on a Greyhound bus opened and some guy with a Smokey the Bear hat stepped on and told a bunch of us that we had three heartbeats to get off his damned bus. I remembered it like it was yesterday. There were twenty-six of us on the bus and we all hustled to get off. The guy in the Smokey hat was joined by three others, all yelling orders at the same time in a common tone and theme.

"Fall in!"

"Line up!"

"Stand on those yellow footprints!"

It'd been a great ride, but now I was ready to move on with my life. I'd given twenty years of it to the Corps, had the opportunity to lead and be led by some of the greatest people I've ever known. The years of service and dozens of deployments had taken their toll. My first marriage lasted six years and we had two beautiful daughters. They left me while I was deployed to Panama. My second marriage lasted only nine months and thankfully there were no kids produced with that shrew. I'd been shot at and blown up, but I'd survived.

Taking my usual seven minute shower, I dressed in my clean and pressed utility uniform, in three. Habits born of necessity are hard to break. Eleven minutes after rising from my bunk I was out the door. I'd packed everything I owned the night before into a single seabag. I traveled light the last few years.

It was a short walk to the mess hall, where I joined other Marines from the several units clustered around the First Battalion, Eighth Marines headquarters, waiting in line for breakfast. Looking around, I saw my platoon sergeant and a few other single noncoms sitting at a table in the corner and walked towards them.

"Mind if I have my last Marine Corps breakfast with you guys?"

"Sure, Gunny," my platoon sergeant, Manuel Ortiz said. "We'd be proud to have you join us. Today's the big day, huh?"

"Yeah," I replied taking a seat. "Transferring to the First Civ Div in about an hour." I talked with the three of them while we ate and drank coffee.

After breakfast I went to my office at the Force Recon building. It was still very early, not even zero-six-hundred yet. As usual, there were only three people there, the Duty Officer from the night before, his driver and a young Lance Corporal who was the new S-4 Clerk. S-4 is the logistical office of a Marine unit. I said good morning to the Duty Officer, a young Second Lieutenant by the name of Scott Briggs, nodded to the Duty Driver, a young PFC I'd never met and then went into the S-4 Office.

"Morning, Gunny," said Lance Corporal Michael Jaworsky. "I figured you'd be stopping in this morning. Want me to make an airline reservation home for you?"

I'd been thinking this over for a week already. I was *leaving* home, not going home. The Corps had been my home and my family for a long time now. The house I grew up in as a kid was owned by my grandparents and I sold it last year, after Mam and Pap passed away. Outside of my room at the BEQ, I didn't really have a home.

"No," I said. "No airline. Can you rent me a car? One way to south Florida?"

He opened a folder on his desk, looked at it and asked, "One way car rental to Fort Myers?"

"Souther than that," I said with a grin and a bumpkin accent. "See if you can find one I can turn in somewhere in the Middle Keys. I know there's an airport in Marathon and another in Key West."

"The Keys? Wow, now that's what I call retiring. I'll see what I can do. Any preference in what kind of car? Need a lot of luggage space? An SUV maybe?"

I laughed and said, "That'd be overkill for my seabag and uniform bag. How about something sporty? Maybe a convertible?"

"I'll let you know in an hour," Jaworsky replied.

I really didn't have a whole lot of work to do. I'd already checked out at the Battalion Adjutants office in S-1, the medical office, dental, checked in my weapons at the armory, and received my new ID card from the S-2 clerk. There were only a few things in my office that I wanted to keep. Pictures and awards hanging on the walls and a few things in my desk drawers.

As if he'd read my mind, Jaworsky knocked on the door frame and came in with a small cardboard box. "Thought you might need this, Gunny."

"Thanks, Mike," I said as I placed the box on my empty desk. He stood in front of it, with his hands clasped behind his back. "Is there something else? No way you got me a car that fast."

"Working on it, Gunny. I just wanted to say it's been an honor working with you."

I stepped out from behind the desk and extended my hand. "It's been a pleasure, Mike."

He shook my hand, then turned and left the office. As I started collecting my belongings and boxing them up, several others dropped in to say goodbye. In fact, nearly everyone in Recon, from the newest Private, to the Battalion Sergeant Major and Commanding Officer, dropped by over the next hour.

The Company CO came by, just as the Battalion CO was leaving. Captain Tom Broderick and I'd known each other for ten years, since he was a wet behind the ears Second Lieutenant, fresh out of Officer Candidate School.

He was due to be promoted to Major next week and would be transferring out after that. At just thirty-two, he was on the fast track to getting a star on his collar. He was six feet tall, a muscular two-hundred pounds, with a shaved head and skin as dark as ebony.

"Really hate to see you go, Jesse."

"I'm having a hard time believing it's been twenty years already, Tom." In front of other Officers and the troops, I'd call him by his rank. But, we'd become close friends and when it was just the two of us, we used first names.

"Been a lot of water under the keel, hasn't it?"

"Yeah, I suppose it has.' I replied. "Have a seat."

We sat down and with a half grin, he said, "I can't stay long, I have a few last minute details to iron out on some douchebag's retirement ceremony."

We talked for a few minutes over coffee then he had to leave. I was just putting the last things in the box when Jaworsky knocked on the door frame again and stepped inside.

"How's a red Mustang convertible sound, Gunny?"

I grinned. "Sounds a whole lot better than a silver bird. Where do I pick it up?"

"It'll be delivered in an hour," he replied puffing his chest out just a little. "One way to Marathon, with a turn-in date four days from today."

"Delivered? Now that's service. Thanks a lot, Mike."

He left then and I glanced at my watch. It'd been a Christmas gift from my wife and oldest daughter many years ago. That brought on a flood of regret.

At a usual retirement ceremony, the Corps has a junior NCO escort the wife to stand alongside her husband, where she's given an award for putting up with his, and the Corps', shit for twenty years. And the retiree's daughters are given a bouquet of flowers. I wouldn't have that.

The Corps was my only family now. I'd spoken with Tom several weeks earlier and asked for a simple ceremony at morning formation.

It was zero-seven-hundred, time to fall in. I picked up my little box of mementos and stood for a moment looking around the office. I poured one last cup of coffee into my heavy porcelain Force Recon mug and headed out the door. I talked to a couple of the office people while downing my last cup of Marine Corps coffee, then leaving the box and mug at the Clerk's desk in front, I walked outside.

The formation was already mustering. My platoon was Scout/Snipers and we usually formed up off to the side of Weapons and Headquarters Platoons. Today, they were formed up in the center, Sergeant Ortiz standing at the front of the loose formation.

As I approached, Sergeant Ortiz ordered the men to attention. Then he did an about face and said, "Scout/Sniper Platoon present or accounted for, Gunny."

I stood in front of Ortiz and looked over the group of men with mixed emotions, making eye contact with every one of them, even though they were supposed to be looking straight ahead. I nodded to them, then looked at my Sergeant.

"Sergeant Ortiz! For the last time! Post!" He smartly did a right face and marched to his position at the head of First Squad.

Looking over my troops once more, I gave the command, "At ease!" With my hands clasped behind my back, I said. "Men, it's been an honor and a privilege to be your leader. I only hope that some of what I tried to teach you shit-birds stuck."

A chorus of grunts and "Oorah!" went up from the platoon and many laughed. Some of these guys, I'd served with in other units and many had been here as long as me. There were a few new guys, who nervously laughed, also.

From behind me came a booming voice that was both strange and familiar at the same time. "Company!"

I snapped to attention as a few whispers came from my platoon. I did an about face and shouted over my shoulder, "Platoon!" My platoon immediately assumed the parade rest position.

Ten paces in front of me stood an old and very close friend and a legend in the Marine Corps, Master Gunnery Sergeant Owen 'Tank' Tankersley, dressed as usual in the Charlie uniform, green trousers and khaki blouse. Tank had been my Platoon Sergeant when I first arrived in the Fleet and was later my Company Gunny. He rarely wore utilities, because on the top of his ribbon rack sat a pale blue ribbon with five white stars, the Medal of Honor.

"A-ten-shun!" boomed Tank and about a hundred pairs of heels came together in unison as the whole company snapped to the position of attention.

"You didn't think I'd miss this, did you, Jesse?" Tank asked quietly.

"It's an honor to have you here, Master Guns."

Tank nodded, then performed an about face and waited as the Battalion Commanding Officer, Lieutenant Colonel Arthur Brooks, strode toward him. The CO stopped two paces in front of Tank, everyone waiting. As is customary, the CO saluted Tank first, in deference to that little blue ribbon.

Tank sharply returned the salute and said, "Alpha Company is formed, sir!"

"Post!" barked Brooks and Tank did a left face and marched around the CO to take his position behind and to his left.

The Battalion CO looked over the three platoons, comprising just one of the Companies under his command, until his gaze finally came to rest on me.

"Good morning, Gunnery Sergeant McDermitt."

"And a fine Marine Corps morning to you, sir," I replied. Brooks and I went back a few years and I'd invited him to personally retire me. Normally, Tom would be commanding the formation as the Company CO.

"Gunnery Sergeant Jesiah Smedley McDermitt," he shouted. "Front and center!"

I winced at the use of my full given name. My Mom's parents were Jewish and insisted on a Jewish name. Both my Dad and Pap were Marines, Pap having served before and during World War Two and once served under the command of one of the Corps' greatest heroes, Smedley Butler, just before the General retired.

I marched forward and came to attention two paces in front of the Battalion Commanding Officer, saluted and said, "Gunnery Sergeant McDermitt, reporting as ordered, sir."

He returned my salute then looked over his left shoulder and barked, "Adjutant! Report!"

A young Captain who had just transferred in from Two-Four stepped forward with several thin, red binders. He opened the first one and began reading. It was a citation from the President of the United States, awarding me the Meritorious Service Medal. When he'd finished reading it, he stepped forward and handed the red binder and a small case to Tank, who opened the case and presented it to the CO.

Brooks took the medal from the case and pinned it onto the pocket flap of my camouflage blouse. Then Tank handed him the red binder and the CO handed it to me. Shaking my right hand as he did so, he said, "Congratulations, Gunny."

The Adjutant read again. My certificate of retirement and transfer to the Marine Corps Reserve. Again, Tank handed the CO a red binder and he handed it to me, shaking hands once more.

The Adjutant then read letters of congratulations from the Commandant and the Sergeant Major of the Marine Corps. I received them with yet another handshake.

It was at this point that the wife and family are usually recognized. Tank looked at me with a sad smile as the CO said quietly, "It's been an honor serving with you Gunny. I know your service has come with great cost. Your nation thanks you."

I saluted and said, "Thank you, sir."

He returned my salute then nodded to the Adjutant, before he and Tank did a right face and marched off to the side of the formation.

Stepping forward, the Adjutant announced, "The formation will now be turned over to Gunnery Sergeant McDermitt, so that he may give his final Marine Corps order."

I took two paces forward, stopped, executed an about face, and looked once more at my platoon. Then I looked left and right, to the men in the other two platoons, many of whom I'd worked closely with over the years. My gaze fell back to the warriors in front of me.

"Company!" I shouted.

Sergeant Ortiz and the other two Platoon Sergeants shouted, "Platoon!"

"Fall Out!" I ordered then turned and walked away toward a large pine tree. There I stopped and was soon joined by Tank, Ortiz, Tom and all the men from my platoon.

Slaps on the back, handshakes, and congratulations were offered, along with many young men thanking me for leading and teaching them. One by one, the troops drifted away until it was just Tank, Tom and me standing in the early morning shade.

"You did good, Jesse," Tank offered. "One day, God forbid, some of these men will owe their lives to you."

"Just doing the job, the way you taught me, Tank." I shook his hand and turned to Tom.

"Thanks, Jesse," Tom said shaking my hand. "If it weren't for you, I wouldn't be half the officer I am today. If there's anything I can ever do for you, let me know."

Just then a red Mustang convertible rounded the corner and parked at the curb in front of the building. A young kid got out and started toward the main entrance before seeing us. He stopped and asked, "You guys know where I can find a Jesse McDermitt?"

CHAPTER ONE

Driving south on US-1 out of Homestead, I turned left onto Card Sound Road. I'd been driving since early morning, having spent the night in a cheap motel south of Jacksonville. Fighting my way through Miami traffic during an afternoon rainstorm had sapped what little patience I had left. Now that I was clear of that hell-hole and about to enter the only tropical destination in the United States, I felt like celebrating. A blackened grouper sandwich at *Alabama Jack's* was in order. It had been far too long since I last enjoyed fresh seafood.

I knew this wasn't going to be an easy transition. Yesterday morning, I was a Marine Gunnery Sergeant, a sniper instructor in charge of over fifty warriors. Today I'm more or less an unemployed drifter, with no real job skills. Unless you count shooting bad people from half a mile away a job skill. Regardless, I was excitedly looking forward to my new life as a civilian. I hadn't even bothered to shave this morning.

I'd called an old friend, James "Rusty" Thurman, several weeks ago, told him of my pending retirement and asked what the job market was like in the Florida Keys. Rusty and I had served together early in my career, but he'd left the Corps after four years, when his wife died in childbirth. One of the few real Conchs left in the Keys, he'd taken over his dad's bar, enlarged it and was planning to offer food in addition to cold beer and liquor. I'd been down there quite a few times over the ensuing years and loved the laid back lifestyle of the islanders.

"Job market?" he'd asked. "Nobody in the Keys has a job, bro. We hustle. Just get your ass down here and we'll figure out what kind of hustle best suits you."

Approaching the toll bridge, I pulled off the two lane road into the parking lot of *Alabama Jack's*, killed the engine on the rental car and headed inside. The place was nearly empty, it being a Wednesday that was to be expected. What few people there were, were either bikers or fishermen. I sat down at a table overlooking the canal where several pelicans looked up expectantly.

"Cold beer, Captain?" a waitress asked, jarring me from my thoughts, while looking out over the canal to the marsh beyond.

I looked up at a pretty brunette in her mid-twenties, with dark brown eyes and a ready smile. "Yeah," I said. "Red Stripe and a blackened grouper sandwich."

As she turned to put my order in, I wondered to myself why she'd called me Captain. A moment later she brought my beer, condensation dripping down the sides of the bottle, and placed it on two napkins.

"Fishing or diving?" she asked.

"I'm sorry?"

"You're a charter Captain, right? The other waitress and I have a bet, whether you're a fishing or dive boat Captain."

"How much is the bet?" I asked, thinking she might just have given me an idea.

"Ten bucks," she said. "And on a slow day like this, it'll probably be more than both our tips."

I laughed and said, "Well, you both lose."

"You're not a charter Captain? We were both sure."

"Fishing and diving," I lied. Maybe one day, though.

I ate my lunch with enthusiasm. Growing up in Fort Myers, we always had fresh fish. My grandparents had raised me since I was eight years old and Pap was a first rate fisherman.

I'd forgotten how good fresh seafood could be, knowing that just a few hours earlier the fish was swimming around, without a care in the world.

I finished eating, paid my tab, including a generous tip, and got back in the rental car. I now had only three days to return it. That's how long I had to find something to drive. Back on the road, I paid the toll for the bridge and came to a complete stop at the top of the high arch. There wasn't any traffic either way, so I put the top down on the Mustang and stood up. Card Sound Bridge is very high and from the top you can see for miles. On a clear day, you can actually see all the way across northern Key Largo to the ocean. Not today, though. It was overcast to the south, but to the northeast, I could see Biscayne Bay. I took a long, deep breath of sea air before continuing.

For the next hour and a half I drove through the upper and middle Keys, the familiar islands and bridges rolling by as I chased the sun west. Pap brought me down here many times as a kid and the drive was always something we both looked forward to. He and Mam passed away just a couple of years ago, within months of each other. I was overseas when she passed. Pap waited until I got home so we could spread her ashes on the upper Peace River, another favorite place.

I finally arrived in Marathon. It had changed a little since I was last here, but not a lot. I slowed as I passed the airport, not exactly sure where the driveway to Rusty's house was. As I was looking for it on the left, an old tank of a car parked at the *Wooden Spoon Restaurant* caught my eye. It had a "For Sale" sign taped inside the windshield. I braked hard, turned in, and parked next to it. It was an old International Travelall that looked like it'd seen a lot. I walked inside and asked who owned it. The waitress said it was the cook's and went to get him.

A Jamaican man came out of the kitchen and said they were slow just now and took me outside to look closer. We haggled over the price and finally agreed on eight hundred dollars.

"Do you know where the *Rusty Anchor* is?" I asked him.

"Sure, mon. Just a quarter mile down Useless One."

I pulled out a roll of bills and handed him a hundred. "I'm staying with Rusty for a day or two. When you finish your shift, stop by and I'll give you the rest and a lift home. Bring the title."

We shook hands and I went on to Rusty's house. As I pulled into the crushed shell driveway and slowly drove under the canopy of overhanging oak, gumbo limbo, and casuarinas, I felt like I'd finally come home.

I parked the car, put up the top and the windows, and grabbed my seabag out of the trunk. After twenty years in the Corps, everything I owned still fit in a single seabag. Well, except for two cleaned and pressed uniforms in a carrier. I'd had a lot more things a couple of times, but two divorces took care of those material possessions.

I slung my seabag over my left shoulder and walked toward the bar. It was mid-afternoon, but there were already a handful of pickups in the parking lot. I pulled open the door and stepped inside, waiting a moment for my eyes to adjust to the darker interior before walking over to the bar. There were five men sitting at the bar and a couple of the tables and all of them turned to look at me, appraising the new stranger. I'd walked into many bars like this, all over the world. Places where working men gather after a hard day. Places where men sized one another up purely on physical characteristics. One by one, they all turned their eyes back to whatever they were looking at before I walked in.

I walked over to the bar, dropped my seabag at the end and took the last stool. The bartender had her back to me polishing the heavy mahogany top.

When she turned around I realized it was Rusty's daughter, Julie. I hadn't seen the girl in over three years. She was just an awkward thirteen year old then, all knobby knees and way too tall for her age.

She looked at me questioningly. "Can I get you something?"

I grinned. "Yeah, Jules. You can tell that old Jarhead in the back he's about to get his ass kicked."

That put ten eyes back on me in an instant and more than one chair leg scraped the floor. Islanders are tight and Rusty was one of them. I was an outsider, a mainlander. Suddenly, a glimmer of recognition lit her eyes.

"Uncle Jesse!" She flew around the end of the bar and leaped into my arms. "Dad said you'd be coming, but he didn't know when."

I set her back on her feet, pushed her back and looked at her. She wasn't an awkward thirteen year old anymore. She was nearly a full grown woman, though she'd just turned seventeen.

"If it weren't for you having your momma's hair, I never would have recognized you, Jules." I stepped back. "Look at you. You're all grown up now. Can we lose the 'uncle' thing, though? A beautiful young woman calling me that makes me feel like I should be playing shuffleboard in Miami, wearing condo commando garb."

She blushed as the men in the bar went back to their conversations. "It's really good to see you again," she said as she went behind the bar. "Dad's out back, fixing up that old shack for our new cook. Want a beer before you go back there?"

"Nice to see you again, too. Make it four Red Stripes. A new cook you say?"

"Yeah, an old Jamaican man who just came to town. Dad's going to let him live in the shack as part of his pay." She took a small cooler from under the bar, filled it with ice, added six bottles from the cooler and handed it to me. "That storm will be on us in a few minutes, y'all might want a couple of extras to ride it out."

As I bent down to pick up my seabag, she stopped me. "Just leave it there, Unc... I mean, Jesse. I'll take it to the house for you." Then she turned to a young man sitting at the bar with two other men. He had long hair and a barely visible mustache. "Watch the bar for me, Jimmy?"

"Sure thing, Julie," he replied with a smile.

I walked through the bar and out the back door with the cooler. The storm front to the south was getting closer as I walked across the sloped backyard toward an old shack. Rusty's grandfather had once used it to make illegal rum during Prohibition. I could hear Rusty swearing at someone or more likely some*thing*. As I stepped onto the small porch of the shack, the first fat drops of rain started hitting the ground around me and pinging on the tin roof.

Rusty and I went through boot camp together at Parris Island in the spring of seventy-nine, riding the same bus together from Jacksonville. We were the only two in our platoon from Florida, so we became fast friends. Later, we served in the same units a couple of times, once at Camp Lejeune, and again on Okinawa. We kept in touch by mail when we weren't stationed together. We were both two months from either going home or shipping over when his wife went into early labor and tragically died giving birth to Julie. Rusty had almost two months of saved leave and used it to get out early. I shipped over. Julie stayed with his parents until he got home three days later and it's been just the two of them ever since. It was a struggle to say the least, a man raising a little girl alone.

Letting the screen door slam, I said, "Sounds like you could use a cold beer there, Devil Dog." He turned around quickly, belying his stature. At just under five-seven, he tipped the scales at more than three-hundred pounds.

"Jesse, you old wharf rat!" He crossed the room quickly and threw his arms around me, nearly lifting me off the floor. Rusty was always a hugger. "You shoulda called. I'd have picked you up at the airport."

"I rented a car and drove down from North Carolina. Damn good to see you again, old friend."

"It's been way too long. I bet Julie barely recognized you."

"How've you guys been?" I asked opening the cooler.

He pulled two beers from the cooler with his big left hand, reached into his back pocket and quickly popped the caps off with an opener he always carried.

"We're doin' good. Trying to fix this place up some. I hired me a genuine Jamaican chef. How about you? Got a third ex-wife yet?"

I laughed and took a long pull on the cold Jamaican beer. "No way, brother. I'm a confirmed bachelor these days."

He grinned through his thick red beard and arched his eyebrows, forming three lines across the breadth of his forehead, below his bald head. "Well, you came to the right place then. Only women around here are married or fed up with men. But, there's hot and cold running tourist women every weekend that you can play with."

I looked around the old rum making shack. He'd completely gutted the place, moving seventy-five years of clutter out, and slightly used furniture in. Originally, it had been a single room, about eight feet by sixteen feet. He'd added a wall, creating a small living space and a bedroom in back. Where the old still had been, a potbellied stove now sat.

The living area had a window that looked out over the Atlantic Ocean, which now had wind-whipped waves and white caps as far as I could see. The only furnishings were two heavy, leather recliners, a tiered table between them with a reading lamp. On either side of the window were two bookcases, already filled with hardback and paperback books.

I glanced through the doorway to see a single bed against the wall and an identical table and lamp next to it. "Pretty sparse living conditions," I noted.

"Rufus, he's my new chef, he said that this was all he wanted. He's an old guy, not sure how old, but he still gets around like a teenager. Used to be head chef at a fancy place down on Jamaica. His wife died a year ago and this is how he wanted to retire. Sit and read by the sea."

Rusty plopped his considerable girth into one of the recliners. "Take a load off, brother."

Sitting back in the recliner, looking out the window at the gray menacing sea, I reached over with my beer bottle and Rusty extended his, clinking the necks together. The storm built in intensity, the heavy rain pinging on the tin roof sounding like a fusillade of automatic weapons fire.

"Got any plans?" Rusty asked.

"Yeah, as a matter of fact I do. Would you think I was totally nuts if I said I wanted to buy a charter boat?"

He nearly choked on his beer and used the bottle to point out the window. "You want to go out on *that*? Hauling some dumbass Yankee bubbas out there to catch fish? That your idea of a hustle?"

I followed his gaze out the window. "Not so much the bubba part, but it'd solve a couple problems. One, I'd have my own place to live and two, if I don't like my neighbor, I can just start the engine and move. What's it take to get a charter license?"

"You're serious?"

"Yeah, I think so. My pension from Uncle Sam is more than enough to cover living expenses and I have quite a bit saved up, plus what Pap and Mam left me. I could buy a really decent boat with that and still have plenty left over."

Rusty took a long pull on his beer. "I was real sorry to hear about their passing. Pap was a smart man and sure could find the fish. And man, could Mam ever cook."

Several times Rusty and I would take leave, or extended weekends together and he'd drop me off in Fort Myers, on his way down here. Most times, Mam would insist on his staying over so he wouldn't have to drive Alligator Alley at night. They treated him like another grandson and it was only natural for him to call them Mam and Pap.

We drank beer, caught up on recent things, reminisced about old times and then he went on to explain the different kinds of licenses and what it'd take to get each, while the storm continued to rage outside. I had to admit, the little cabin certainly had its appeal.

Suddenly, the rain stopped and within seconds the sun was shining, causing steam to rise up from everywhere. "Welcome to Florida, bro. If you don't like the weather, just wait an hour. Let's go up to the bar."

We got up and went out into the sweltering humid air. It was early June, but in the Keys the passage of time is measured by the seasons. Hurricane season and tourist season. Though summer still brought quite a few tourists to the southernmost tip of Florida, winter was the big tourist season.

We walked into the bar, where several more people had taken refuge from the storm. Rusty went behind the bar and yanked the cord on an old brass ship's bell mounted on the wall, getting everyone's attention.

"Folks, this big landlubber is one of my best friends in the whole world, Jesse McDermitt. We served together in the Corps and he's just retired. Says he wants to buy a charter boat."

Rusty pointed people out and gave me all their names. The young man with the long hair was Jimmy Saunders. Seated next to him were two guys about my age, Al Fader, and Charlie Hofbauer and a tall black guy, Sherman Crawford. The four of them were shrimpers out of Key West, Rusty explained.

After the introductions were made, Sherman spoke up, surprising me with an Australian accent. "Fishing or diving charter, mate?"

"Maybe a little of both," I replied. "Very little though. More than anything, I want a boat I can live on and big enough I can go exploring."

Jimmy turned to Al and pointed to the end of the bar. "Hand me that paper you were just looking at, Skipper."

Al shoved it down the bar and Jimmy spun it around, pointing to an ad for a Coast Guard auction in Miami scheduled for the following Saturday. Circled under the banner was a listing for a boat. Jimmy tapped the picture with his finger. "Dude, if you want to do a little of both and want a really cool place to live when you're not doing either, right here's the boat you want." Then he grinned at Rusty and turned back to me. "Hope your credit's good, man. That's a lot of samolians."

I looked down at the listing. It had a picture of a sleek looking offshore fishing boat, with wide Carolina bow flares and a long foredeck. The listing said it was a forty-five-foot Rampage convertible and had a reserve of three-hundred-thousand dollars. I spun the paper back to Jimmy. "I don't know a lot about individual boat models, but I know Rampage is about top of the line. What can you tell me about this model?"

He looked at me quizzically. "Top of the line? Yeah, dude. And the forty-five is the company flagship, man. Has a really nice forward stateroom with its own private head. Aft of there is the guest cabin and head. A couple steps up from there to the galley and salon. Rampage goes all out here, man. Really nice woodwork and furniture, even a big screen TV. Step down aft the salon to the cockpit. All business there, dude. Plenty of deck space, storage and fish boxes, fighting chair, even a cleaning station and sink. A hatch amidships takes you down to the engine room, below the salon. The forty-five usually has a pair of C-15 Cats down there. That's eight-hundred and fifty horses each. Plus a water maker, generator, and inverter. A ladder to port takes you up to the bridge, loaded with electronics. Radar, fish finders, sonar and VHF radios. But, it being a Coast Guard auction, this particular boat was probably seized from smug drugglers. Could be shot all to hell, man."

The kid seemed to be pretty knowledgeable. "You busy Saturday?"

"You think you can afford a boat like that, dude?"

"If it doesn't go much over the reserve, yeah, I can afford it." What I didn't say and what was nobody's business was that when Pap died, I was his only heir. He'd started an architecture firm after World War Two, was very successful, and sold it about five years ago for over two million dollars.

"Count me in," Rusty said. "I'll drive you up there and if you buy it, Jimmy here can help you pilot it back and get your sea legs wet. If not, we can always go to a nudie show on South Beach."

Jimmy thought it over a minute. "Okay, you got yourself a first mate, bro."

The front door of the bar opened then and the cook from the Wooden Spoon walked in. He looked around, his eyes adjusting to the darkness and spotted me and walked over. "Got your ride outside, mon."

"You bought Joe's piece-a-shit, man?" Jimmy asked.

"Not yet, he ain't," the cook said. "Still owes me seven hundred."

I pulled a roll of bills from my pocket and peeled off seven one-hundred-dollar-bills and handed them to the man.

"Got the title, Joe?"

"Ya, mon." He produced the document, signed the back and handed it to me. I stuffed the paper in my back pocket.

Jimmy pointed to the ad again and laughed. "You can afford that boat and bought a piece of crap for seven Benjamins to drive around in?"

"Wouldn't make sense to haul bait and boat parts in a new pickup," I said. "Besides, the car seemed to call my name."

CHAPTER TWO

The International proved to be everything Jimmy had said and then some. I spent another eight hundred bucks on it before the weekend, replacing a water pump, putting in all new plugs, points, condenser, and plug wires and replacing all four tires.

Early Saturday, Jimmy arrived as Rusty and I were eating breakfast in the bar. Rufus had returned from Jamaica with a few personal things and proved to be every bit the cook he claimed to be. We set out for Miami just as the sun was rising over the ocean, clear and bright.

Arriving at the Port of Miami at zero-eight-hundred, I registered with the auction house, provided my bank statement and paid the thousand dollar fee. We went straight from there to the Rampage and checked it out. As it turned out, Jimmy was much more knowledgeable than he'd intimated. The stateroom, guest cabin, heads, galley, and salon were in disarray, but he pointed out what it could look like. On the bridge, he showed me the electronics system, everything he'd mentioned and then some. The radar was top of the line, as were the fish finders. Going down into the engine room, Jimmy let out a low whistle.

"What is it?" I asked from the hatch, gazing at the meticulously clean, white engines.

"These ain't C-15s, man," he said. "Whatever smug druggler owned this must have ordered it special. These here are eighteen liter monsters, over a thousand horses each. This boat'll go forty knots, minimum, dude! Both of 'em have less than eight-hundred hours, too."

We checked out the exterior, as the boat sat on wooden blocks in the huge boatyard. We couldn't find a single bullet hole, or even a crack in the gel coat. The twin propellers were in recessed tunnels and looked nearly new.

"She only draws about four feet at anchor, maybe two on plane," Jimmy explained. "These props are aftermarket, made for speed. She carries seven-hundred gallons of fuel and a hundred gallons of fresh water. But, with that water maker, you can have water any time. Those big ass engines will suck your wallet dry, dude. Probably burns somewhere about sixty or seventy gallons an hour at a cruising speed of twenty-five knots. Probably a hundred gallons at wide open throttle."

Most of the interest from the other people at the auction seemed to be centered on a trio of what's commonly called 'go fast' boats, long, sleek, twin-engine racing boats. Only a couple other men were looking over the Rampage.

Two hours later, it came up on the auction block and the auctioneer started the bidding at two-hundred-thousand. With two men alternating bids, it quickly went up to two-eighty. One of the men bowed out and a third man bid two eighty-five. It went back and forth between those two until it reached three-hundred and twenty-thousand dollars. The third man bowed out and the auctioneer called for any other bids.

When he called a second time, I raised my paddle and shouted, "Three fifty!"

The first bidder looked over at me, with a less than pleased look on his face and raised it to three fifty-five. We went back and forth raising by five thousand until he balked, but finally said, "Three seventy."

I knew I had him then. He hadn't planned to go higher than that. I was ready to go to four-fifty, based on both Rusty and Jimmy's estimate that it was worth at least half a million. It was time to put the other bidder to bed.

"Three hundred and ninety thousand dollars!" The man looked over at me and shook his head, placing his paddle on the chair beside him.

The auctioneer saw the other bidder's defeated look and having no other bids said, "Going once! Going twice! Sold to Captain McDermitt, for three-hundred and ninety thousand!"

I was now the proud owner of a one year old forty-five foot Rampage, worth half a million bucks and a twenty-six year old International four-by-four that probably wasn't worth what I paid for the water pump.

The auction manager quickly came over to us and said, "Congratulations, Captain. There's no charge for putting her in the water and your entry fee is refunded if the winning bid is more than ten-percent over reserve. When will you want to take possession?"

I pulled out my checkbook and said, "Right now. Get her in the water." I never dreamed I'd write a check for that amount, but an hour later, I'd done that and was leaving the dock in my new boat.

Jimmy showed me how to use the engines to maneuver away from the dock, putting one in reverse and the other in forward to make the boat spin sideways. Twenty minutes later, we rounded the tip of Virginia Key into the open Atlantic.

"Switch places, Captain," Jimmy said as he got up from behind the helm. I sat down behind the wheel and took it in my hands. The feeling was indescribable. My own boat. "What do you think you're gonna call her, man?"

"A name?" I asked. "Haven't even thought about it. Hell, until three days ago when a waitress at *Alabama Jack's* said I looked like a charter boat owner, I never even thought of being one."

"You mean to tell me you dropped three-hundred and ninety grand on a *whim*, dude?"

"Think it's too late to get my money back?" I asked as Jimmy reached over and pushed the throttles forward.

The big boat settled down at the stern and lifted those wide bow flares above the wave tops and in seconds we were skimming across the chop, which was hardly noticeable. The exhilaration I felt as she surged up onto plane was almost like that of being in combat. Different, but just as intense. We called it 'the jazz'.

Jimmy looked at me and said, "Yep, sure is. The worm done turned, man."

I grinned at him and made a wide, sweeping turn in forty foot deep water to the south. "Keep her a mile off Key Biscayne there," he said. "There's nothing but deep water all the way to Marathon, so long as you stay a mile off the reef line."

I looked down at the GPS, which showed we were traveling at twenty-eight knots. I reached for the throttles. "Why don't we see what she's got?"

I pushed the throttles all the way forward and the big boat surged ahead, delivering much more power and acceleration than I would have thought possible. A moment later, the knot meter showed a speed of forty-two knots.

"We're bucking a fifteen knot head wind," Jimmy shouted. "Once we make the turn down at Key Largo and have the wind on our beam, I guarantee you she'll reach forty-five knots, dude. Hey, you mind if I smoke?"

I'd never picked up the smoking habit, but never begrudged those who did. To me, it was a sign of weakness, but that's just me. "Go ahead," I said. He reached into his pocket and pulled out a plastic bag and a pack of rolling papers.

"Pot?" I asked and grabbed the bag from his hands. Without a seconds hesitation I tossed the bag overboard. "Are you fucking nuts?"

"Dude! That was a hundred bucks of primo weed!"

I thought it over for a second and said, "Look, I'll pay you back. But no pot on my boat. No way. Ever. I can't tell you how to run your life, but on my boat, no way. For all we know, this boat might have been confiscated from the previous owner for having no more than that on board."

"That's harsh, man. It's more than two hours to Marathon."

"Four," I said as I pulled the throttles back to twenty-five knots. "I'm sorry, Jimmy. Maybe I overreacted. I'll be straight with you. I don't care what a man does on his own time, but I hired you to help me get this boat to Marathon."

"You didn't hire me, dude. I volunteered to help you out, that's all. Only reason I did was because Julie likes you."

"Well, let's take care of first things first," I said reaching into my pocket. I handed him four crisp one hundred dollar bills and said, "You're hired."

"A days wage for a mate is only two-hundred."

"The other two-hundred is to replace your pot and doing the boat survey. I'm serious though. If you ever come on my boat again, leave the pot in your car."

"Fair enough, man."

"Now what's this about Julie?"

He went on to explain how he'd had a crush on her since she was in ninth grade, even though he was several years older. She'd never shown any interest in boys and never went out with anyone. She went fishing with the guys and was a better fisherman than any of them, but none had even gotten to first base.

"How long have you known her?" he asked.

"All her life," I replied. "Rusty and I went through Boot Camp together in seventy-nine. I was his best man when he married Julie's mom. First time I met her, she was only three days old. I came down here with Rusty, when her mom died."

"You have kids?"

"Two daughters from my first marriage. Haven't seen them in a few years. Their mom moved them back up north."

We rode on in silence for a while and gradually started talking about boats, fishing, and local waters. Jimmy was born and raised in the Keys and seemed to know the water on both sides of the island chain as well as any man.

"How much do you make shrimping?" I asked.

"On a good week, about six-hundred. Most weeks only about four, though. Why?"

"Well, if I'm gonna do any chartering, I'll need some help. I thought you said a mate makes two-hundred a day."

"I'm just a deckhand on the shrimp boat. Al Fader's my boss."

"I'll pay you four-hundred a week, if you come to work for me and an extra two hundred a day every day we go out on the water. Might be slow at first, but I think we can drum up a couple of charters a week easy enough, just by putting a shingle on the dock behind this boat."

"Yeah, she's a head turner that's for sure. You're serious about a job, man?"

"Only if you leave the weed on shore, yeah."

He extended his hand and I took it. "You got a mate, bro. So, what about that name? Rusty said you were from Fort Myers?"

"Yeah, so?"

"You know Gasparilla Island?"

"Sure, I grew up just across Charlotte Harbor from there. What about it?"

"Did you know it's named after a famous pirate?"

Though I knew the story, I let him tell me about the English pirate, Jose Gaspar and how he went down with his ship after mistaking the USS Enterprise for a merchant ship.

"So, a man from Fort Myers buys a boat with no name," he said. "Intending to make a fortune catching fish? What about *Gaspar's Revenge*?"

"I like it. *Gaspar's Revenge*. Has a cool ring to it."

"Where you going to dock her, dude?"

I suddenly realized that I had no idea. I should have thought about that before buying it.

"I really don't know. You know some place?"

"Let me make a call," he said, reaching for the mic on the VHF radio. He adjusted the frequency and said into the mic, "This is *MV Gaspar's Revenge* calling *Dockside*. Aaron, do you copy?"

Immediately a voice came back over the radio, "This is *Dockside*. Go ahead *Gaspar's Revenge*."

"Aaron, this is Jimmy. Hey, do you have dock space for a forty-five footer. I'm helping out a new charter Captain." Turning to me, he said, "Aaron runs *Dockside Lounge*. They have dockage there for about twenty boats.

"Hi, Jimmy," Aaron replied cheerfully. "Yeah, I have a slip for a forty-five. How long will he be staying?"

Jimmy looked at me and I shrugged. "Permanently, if the price is right."

He keyed the mic and said, "Captain McDermitt is looking for a base to charter his Rampage on a permanent basis."

There was silence for a moment then Aaron said, "Ten dollars a foot per month, includes shore power, water, phone, and cable."

I knew I was being taken. I took the mic from Jimmy and said, "This is Captain Jesse McDermitt. I'll take the slip for a week at two hundred dollars, until I can find a better rate."

There was another moment of silence then Aaron said, "I'm sure I can convince the owner to make a special rate, Captain. When will you be here?"

I looked at my watch and said, "Our ETA is sixteen-hundred."

"Look forward to meeting you, Captain. Slip number ten is at the end, first one you'll come to out of Sister Creek, right next to the dinghy dock and boat ramp. *Dockside* out."

Jimmy burst out laughing. "Man, you're good. His usual rate is eight bucks a foot for semi-permanent. And he doesn't have any big charter boats there. This beauty will bring in more than the dock fee in just beer and food from your clients. Not to mention the fuel, man."

"Okay," I said. "You have three hours to teach me enough to keep from looking like a jackass."

For the next three hours, he described Boot Key Harbor, the Knight Key channel approach on the west side and Sister Creek on the south. He explained how to maneuver the boat outside the slip and back it in, without hitting the piers. He told me everything he knew about charter fishing and diving. By the time we pulled into Sister Creek, I was well armed with knowledge.

Surprisingly, I didn't run over any boats in the harbor and managed to back the *Revenge* into slip ten without taking out the whole dock. Jimmy had explained how to face aft when backing and use the throttles to steer, with nudges to the wheel from my back.

Thirty minutes later, Aaron and I agreed on three hundred a month and he contacted a local air brush artist to come out and put the name on the boat, the gear box, and the portal over the dock. I was now in business. That is, with the exception of getting a six pack license to charter, registering the boat, and acquiring a business license. Details.

CHAPTER THREE

For the next month, Jimmy and I got the boat ready to charter, made arrangements with a nearby bait shop, he helped me buy the right tackle and other gear, and went with me to the County Clerk to get a business license and even to the Chamber of Commerce. He suggested I might want to buy a small skiff to get around whenever the International broke down, explaining that just about everything was accessible by boat on the island.

I had to go down to Key West to register the boat and while I was waiting, I looked over some pamphlets that were on the counter.

"Thinking of buying an island?" one of the clerks asked.

"Buy an island?"

"Yes sir," she said. "Some of the smaller uninhabited islands are available to be used as fish camps."

"Really?" I said. "How much would a little island sell for?"

Later that evening, after I'd registered the *Revenge*, Rusty, Jimmy, and I were sitting at a table in the bar, eating blackened grouper and washing it down with cold Kalik beer.

"You bought a freaking island?" Rusty said in amazement.

"It's a little over two acres at high tide," I replied. "Up in the Content Keys, near Harbor Channel. And no, I haven't bought it yet. Just put a deposit on it until I can see it."

He roared with laughter, his face turning beet red. "Bro, most of those islands up there you can't even get a flats skiff up to. You got taken."

"So, are you gonna take me up there, or not?"

"Sure, first thing in the morning," he said still laughing. "Be prepared to do some wading, though."

We left before sunrise and got to the GPS coordinates I was given at the County Clerk's office. Rusty was right. Even though the tide was nearly high, we beached his little skiff a good twenty yards from the mangrove shoreline and only ten yards out of Harbor Channel.

I was somewhat dejected. "Maybe the water's a little deeper on the other side."

"Might be," Rusty said pondering the little island that lay before us. "I don't get up here enough to know for sure. The thing is, if you're serious about buying this island, right here's where you're going to have to dig a channel. That, or a dock all the way out to Harbor Channel."

We got out and waded ashore. The mangroves weren't very thick, but the saw palmetto was. We finally found what looked like a path to the interior and followed it. After only ten yards it opened up into a large clearing, mostly sea grass and a few palmetto, scrub oak, sea grapes, and one tall coconut palm right in the middle.

Rusty looked back through the path where the skiff sat with its anchor line stretched out halfway to shore. Then he looked back to the clearing. To the west was a pretty wide opening through the underbrush, with only a handful of coconut palms and gumbo limbo trees. Beyond it we could see a sandbar twenty yards offshore.

"You know," he said thoughtfully. "If you was to dredge a channel from out there, right up into the island here, you could build a little stilt house above it and have a ladder going right up into the house."

"Why not in the middle of the island?"

"Yeah, that'd work. But, it'd be really cool to park your boat under the house."

As we walked out into the clearing, I was giving what he said some serious thought. We split up and explored the little island, which didn't take long. Before the clearing on the west side overlooking the sandbar we found where someone had a campfire once, a rusty steel fire ring the only sign. Outside of that, there was nothing to indicate anyone had ever been here.

On the north side, the water was deeper. It looked to be about two feet deep just a few yards from shore and dropped to even deeper water twenty yards out. It was surrounded by even shallower water, a natural lagoon.

"I think I'm going to buy it," I blurted out.

"I gotta admit, it's secluded. Didn't you say something about it had to be developed as a fishing lodge or some such?"

"Yeah. Within ten years, I'd have to have an established fish camp, even if it's nothing more than a bunkhouse."

"Lots of fly fishermen come up this way," he said. "A place to overnight wouldn't be a bad idea. Julie'd be the one to talk to about that. I swear, that girl knows every ledge, reef head, and lobster hole from here to Key Weird."

"Was a time when you did, too."

He chuckled. "Long term memory's the first to go." Suddenly, we heard his outboard cranking and we both spun around at the sound.

"Sumbitch!" he exclaimed. "Someone's trying to steal my boat." In a second, he reached under his shirt at his back and pulled out a Sig Sauer nine millimeter semi-automatic and started running across the clearing. It always surprises me how fast he's able to move for a man his size. I tore off after him and we crashed through the saw palmetto on the south end of the island together just in time to see a beat up aluminum johnboat speeding away with two young men in it.

Rusty sloshed out to his skiff and checked it over quickly. "Damn kids," he said. "At least they weren't smart enough to take anything."

"Lucky they didn't get it started," I said. "It's a long swim back to Marathon."

He pulled another key ring out of his pocket. "Luck don't have nothing to do with it. The key in the ignition only spins the starter. This one turns on the ignition."

"Smart thinking."

"There's pirates all over these waters, bro. If I was you Jesse, I'd install a good security system on your boat and never go out without firepower. The more the better."

"Pirates?"

"Not the swashbuckling kind. The drug running kind. They'll board ya, slice your throat, and feed ya to the sharks. Then they'll use your boat to run drugs, or worse."

A month later, the island was mine. I'd also spent several thousand dollars on a state of the art security system for *Gaspar's Revenge*, fishing tackle, dive equipment, and an air compressor for filling scuba tanks. I bought a nice little eighteen foot Maverick Mirage flats skiff from a used boat dealer on Big Pine Key, just across the Seven Mile Bridge. I also invested in armament.

It turned out that Jimmy was sort of a computer guru and set me up with a website to attract clients. Aaron had a friend who created some slick looking flyers that Aaron displayed prominently in the restaurant and bar. I was a charter boat owner and captain.

I took Rusty's warning to heart, especially after a pleasure craft with a family on board was attacked while cruising a few miles off Boca Chica Key. The father was shot and thrown overboard, but he survived. His wife and two teenage daughters disappeared with the boat. I applied for and received a concealed carry permit, which I thought was laughable after twenty years in the Corps. I didn't go anywhere without firepower.

A friend of Rusty's converted the bunk in the forward berth, so the whole thing raised up on hydraulic cylinders. It was equipped with a digital lock to secure it. I bought a large, heavy trunk and put it under the bunk. Inside were watertight boxes that held four Sig P-226's with plenty of ammo and magazines. I even went so far as to special order an M-40A3 sniper rifle, the newer version to the one I used in Somalia several years ago. Bring on the swashbucklers.

Over the summer, I managed to eke out a living without having to dip too much into my savings, which had quickly been cut nearly in half. I really loved being out on the water, but I let Jimmy handle the clients. I learned a lot from him in the first few weeks and soon we made a good team. He kept up his end of the deal and never once brought pot aboard. By the end of summer, we'd earned a reputation as one of the top offshore fishing charter boats in the middle Keys and in high demand. This was mostly due to Jimmy's intimate knowledge of the water. I paid him a fair weekly wage even though we only went out two or three times a week.

During the daylight hours, when we didn't have a charter, I used the little Maverick and scoured the back country north of Marathon and Big Pine Key, sometimes camping out on my island and doing some target practice. I took snorkeling gear and a spear gun on these forays and managed to keep the freezer aboard the *Revenge* stocked with fish fillets, stone crab claws and lobster later in the summer.

In early August, Jimmy and I built a bench rack to replace the fighting chair in the cockpit of the *Revenge*. It was big enough to accommodate six divers sitting back to back and locked in place with a short pole that fit into the fighting chair receiver. Lobster season was upon us and I wanted to take advantage of the influx of divers. They paid more and tipped better.

There were days when I missed the rigid structure and organization I had in the Corps, but I was slowly relaxing and learning to take each day for what it was. I spent some time on the island and using various implements of destruction, I cleared some of the underbrush away in the center. One night, after a particularly hard day of digging and uprooting a number of scrub oaks, I sat in my skiff anchored on Harbor Channel, fishing. The sun had gone down hours before and the moon was only a sliver on the western horizon. As I waited for a grouper to take my bait, I looked up to the night sky.

"Damn," I said aloud to nobody, my voice sounding unusually loud in the darkness. I'd never really noticed the night sky way out here in the back country. It had been a good fifteen minutes since I doused my flashlight and my eyes had become adjusted to the darkness. With no lights around to pollute the sky, I was able to see a lot more stars than I'd ever seen in my life. A hazy streak of stars spread across the inky blackness in an arc from the southwest to the southeast. I knew it was our own galaxy, the Milky Way, but I'd never really seen it so clearly before. It really made me feel small and insignificant.

The next day, having returned to civilization, I related my star gazing experience to Rusty. "Let your eyes get used to the darkness up there and you can see millions of years into the past," he said. "Ya oughta learn to navigate by them. Never know when a skill like that might be needed."

"Millions of years into the past?"

"Sure, them stars ain't nearby, man. Ever heard of a light year? It takes years for the light from the nearest one to get here. That's Rigil Kent, or Alpha Centauri. This time of year, it's visible low on the southern horizon, it and Beta Centauri point to Crux, the Southern Cross. Some of them stars are millions of light years away, so yeah, you're looking into the past when you see their light."

"When did you get to be such a science whiz?" I asked.

He went on to explain how his grandfather had taught him celestial navigation at an early age. "The stars are timeless and predictable, Jesse. If you know them, you'll never get lost. Early mariners had only a compass, a sextant, and a timepiece to navigate and map the world."

So I cheated those early mariners, bought a laptop and started teaching myself about the stars. I found a website that advertised celestial navigation and bought a sextant and star charts. It turned out to not be as daunting as I thought it would be. Locating the North Star and shooting it with the sextant gave a fairly precise latitude. Using the star charts, I could locate and shoot one of the equatorial stars at a certain time of night and that would give me a pretty precise longitude. Combining latitude and longitude, then comparing the location on my nautical charts to the GPS, I found I could quickly determine where I was, within a mile or two.

CHAPTER FOUR

In early September we had a hurricane scare. Or at least I did. Rusty and the other locals took it in stride. Tropical Storm Floyd turned into a hurricane about three-hundred miles east of Puerto Rico and a couple of days later, it was a strong category four storm, plowing through the southeastern Bahamas on a beeline for the Florida Keys. With sustained winds of one-hundred and fifty-five miles per hour, a very low barometric pressure and hourly reports from the Bahamas showing massive damage, I was really worried about the boat.

"You have insurance, right?" Rusty asked when I brought it up Sunday morning.

"Yeah, but I'd rather not have to replace her. She's my home."

"Fuel up and take her out," he said. "But, I'm betting this storm's gonna turn north before it makes Andros."

Andros Island is the largest of the Bahama chain and less than one-hundred and fifty miles from Miami. "Take her out in a hurricane?" I asked incredulously.

"Not in. Before. She can handle rough seas and has plenty enough speed and range to dodge a storm. Hell, bro, you could make the northwest coast of Florida without stopping in less than ten hours."

Monday evening, as people began evacuating coastal areas from Key West to the Outer Banks of North Carolina, I prepared to do just that. I topped the tanks and stocked up on provisions. If the storm didn't turn by morning, I was going to bug out for my hometown of Fort Myers, on the southwest coast.

Leaving at sunrise, I could be there by zero-nine-hundred, refuel and head further north if it looked like Floyd would cross the state. I walked from *Dockside* to the *Anchor* at zero-five-thirty. There were already a lot of people there, glued to the Weather Channel. Julie poured me a cup of coffee when I sat down at the bar next to Jimmy.

"It started turning northward about an hour ago," Julie said. "They're forecasting it to skirt the coast about a hundred miles off the northern part of the state and make landfall in the Carolinas in a couple of days, or maybe even turn out to sea."

"Where is it now?" I asked.

Coming through the back door Rusty said, "About a hundred and forty miles east of Andros. Turning north like I said it would."

"So you're an astronomer *and* a meteorologist now?" I asked turning toward him.

"No, I'm a Conch." He placed a case of Budweiser on the bar and started stocking the cooler. "My dad was a Conch, his dad was a Conch and his dad before him. Julie here is fifth generation Conch. When a people live this close to the sea for over a hundred years, they pick up a thing or two about it."

"No chance it'll turn back this way then?"

"None," he replied as he continued putting beer in the coolers behind the bar. "Did ya feel the air this morning walking over?"

"Feel the air?"

"Yeah. Feel the air. Go outside and do it right now."

I got up and walked out the door and stood in the middle of the yard on the side of the bar, just as the sky to the east was starting to get a purple glow. Rusty walked quietly up beside me. It always amazed me how a man of his size could move without making a sound.

"A light westerly wind, cool and dry," he said. "Ya feel it?"

Before I could answer he continued, "But a heaviness to the air. Sound travels better, you can pick up that morning dove way on the other side of the woods. Hear it?"

"Yeah," I replied.

"Dense air means high pressure. A 'cane wants to avoid high pressure, but at the same time wants to feed off it, drawing the air toward it. She prefers to feed on warm, moist air, though. So, she'll move away from cool, dry air. Been this way a couple days now. Ya just gotta think like a storm, my brother."

"I have a lot to learn master, before I'll be a Conch."

As we turned back toward the bar he said, "Being a Conch is a birthright. But, you'll make a decent waterman one day. Listen to that hippy ya got workin' for ya. Even when he's high as a kite, he knows more about being a waterman than most of the Conchs round here. Boy seems to be in tune with the sky and the water."

Coming from Rusty, I decided that was high praise. We'd had two dive charters scheduled for the day. The morning one had canceled and I told Jimmy to cancel the afternoon one, too. He'd protested, but I told him to do it anyway. Now, I wish I'd listened to him.

We went back inside and Julie poured me another cup of coffee. Turning to Jimmy I said, "You think you might be able to get that afternoon charter back?"

"Won't need to, man," he replied with a knowing grin. "I figured you'd come around, so I didn't cancel. Them guys have been diving down here for years and woulda booked someone else within thirty minutes."

"We're still on?"

"Yeah, man. They'll be at the dock at noon. I could call 'em and see if they wanna go out earlier, if ya want."

"Do it," I said. "And from now on, you handle all the scheduling. But, no more than three work days a week."

Julie handed Jimmy a cordless phone, while he dug through his pockets for the number. Within a few minutes, he'd moved the charter up to zero-nine-thirty and booked the same four guys for an afternoon and night dive, also.

"You'll like these guys, man," he said. "They're hard core divers." While I had no idea what that meant, I believed him.

"Ya need to make a plan," Rusty said. "One day a 'cane will come and if ya ain't ready, ya could lose everything. I know you're always well stocked with provisions and ya got that water maker, but what would you do if and when the real thing comes?"

"Probably do like you said and head out, though I'm not crazy about the idea."

"Ya never know what a storm'll do, though," he continued. "If you go north, it might just chase you all the way to Pensacola. Then you'd be out several hundred bucks of fuel and still be facing the storm."

"What would you suggest then?"

"Head for a hurricane hole, dude" Jimmy suggested.

Rusty nodded. "Yep, a deep water creek with lots of mangroves you can tie off to."

I thought it over. "What's wrong with Boot Key Harbor?"

"It'll do for a small storm," Rusty began. "But a big blow can have a storm surge higher than Boot Key. Then that harbor'll just be a part of the Atlantic. Me and my dad got caught in a bad one, when I was a kid. We were out in Florida Bay fishing. He drove that old trawler straight up Shark River to Tarpon Bay."

"I know that area," I said.

"Thought you would. Tarpon Bay is plenty wide and deep. In a big blow there'll be some sizable waves even in the bay. But, there's a ton of deep water creeks that feed into it. Stock up on a bunch of long, heavy lines, to tie her off to the mangroves and any of those would be a dandy hurricane hole."

Jimmy and I went back to the boat and got things ready for the charter. I planned to head for the marina store when we got back and do just as Rusty had suggested. The four men arrived early and we were headed out to the reef before zero-nine-thirty.

They wanted to do a deep dive first and specifically asked to dive the Thunderbolt. She's an old Navy cable layer that Florida Power and Light later used to study lightning, hence her name. She was scuttled in eighty-six just five miles southeast of Marathon in one hundred-fifteen feet of water. Jimmy had taken me out there just a few weeks earlier and I was amazed at the amount of life that had accumulated on her in thirteen years. Between the two huge props we saw a large Jewfish, probably five feet long and four-hundred pounds. He told me after the dive that the fish 'lived' there and was a popular attraction.

Jimmy was right. After meeting the four men, I liked them immediately. Three were retired military like myself and had thousands of dives logged in their books. The fourth was a friend who was a fairly new diver, but about the same age.

The Thunderbolt dive went well, but at one-hundred-twenty feet they only had about fifteen minutes of bottom time and still needed to take a ten minute safety stop at the submerged buoy, which was actually an aluminum beer keg. Once everyone was back on board I motored slowly northeast toward the reef line.

There was no hurry, since the divers needed a long surface interval after making the deep dive to the screws of the Thunderbolt to see the giant Jewfish. I dropped the anchor in a sandy spot near a reef called Coffins Patch for the second dive.

I'd been on this reef many times, myself. I knew it would be a great dive for the men, especially the new diver. It's loaded with pillar coral, some reaching a height of five or six feet, and dozens of species of tropical fish.

A Spanish galleon, the *Ignacio*, had wrecked on the reef in a hurricane in the early seventeen-hundreds, but hardly anything remained of the wreck to see. She carried silver and gold coins, though. So, divers were always fanning the sand in search of an elusive piece-of-eight or doubloon.

Being only twenty-five feet at the deepest, the divers were down well over an hour, only surfacing when the new diver was low on air. We got them back on board and I invited them into the salon, while Jimmy hooked their tanks up to the compressor to refill. We had lunch and talked about diving and of course our time in the service. I was surprised to learn that Jimmy had served three years in the Navy.

After lunch, I offered to take the divers west to Looe Key for a dusk and night dive. They jumped at the chance, since most dive operators preferred to keep the distance between dives to a minimum and Looe Key was southwest of Big Pine Key, about thirty miles from Coffins Patch. Plus, it offered plenty of extra surface time, to bleed off the nitrogen that had built up in their bodies. Both Looe Key and Coffins Patch were inside the sanctuary, so they couldn't take any lobster. They were planning to do some lobster diving the next day in the back country, anyway.

We arrived at Looe Key an hour before sunset. The divers having spent a good three hours on the surface, could now start at the offshore edge of the finger reef in one hundred feet and work toward the shallows. Even though it was still daylight, at a hundred feet it would be nearly pitch dark, so they all carried high powered, underwater flashlights and backups. Two of the divers also carried expensive underwater digital camera equipment. Jimmy had loaded editing software on my laptop computer just for digital photography and offered to help the divers review and enhance their pictures. That was a big hit with the two photographers.

Jimmy had been keeping track of their dive times and surface intervals on the laptop, even though the three experienced divers had underwater dive computers strapped to their wrists. Before entering the water, they compared all four and unanimously decided to go with the most conservative profile and limit the first dive to twenty minutes.

Since there were no mooring buoys this far off the reef, I told them I'd move due east of where we dropped them, tie off to a buoy in thirty feet of water and switch on the powerful underwater lights that the *Revenge* had mounted on the transom, below the water line.

It was nearly twenty-one-thirty when we got back to *Dockside*. Jimmy helped the divers edit their pictures and showed them a few things his new software could do, while I started hosing down the foredeck. When they left, each of the four divers gave Jimmy a fifty-dollar tip and assured me they'd not only spread the word, but would be calling again soon.

While hosing down the deck in the cockpit and rinsing the equipment, I turned to Jimmy. "You're editing software was a big hit. Got any other high tech ideas like that?"

"How about an upgraded sound system, dude? Maybe some underwater speakers?"

"Yeah, a better stereo maybe. I don't know about underwater heavy metal, though."

I told Jimmy to go ahead on home and I finished cleaning the boat myself. Eating a late supper, I sat on the bridge with a few cold Jamaican Red Stripe beers in a small cooler. My slip was next to the dinghy dock and far enough away from *Dockside* that the sounds from inside were pretty muted, but close enough that I could see the goings on outside.

There were about forty boats of all shapes and sizes moored in Boot Key Harbor, even a Japanese junk. All of the liveaboards in the harbor used the dinghy dock to come and go. *Dockside* provided a mail slot for each of the liveaboards and free use of the showers, all for only fifty dollars a month. Not a bad way to live if you're on the cheap.

A dinghy was rowing toward the docks, with three people aboard, nearly overloading it. As they neared the dock I could tell it was a man and two women that I hadn't seen around before. I didn't notice what boat they'd come from. As the man tied off the little boat, the women stepped out, each carrying a bag. As they walked by, I couldn't help but notice they were both very attractive and dressed expensively. After they walked on toward the bar the man climbed out and started after them, but he didn't seem to be in much of a hurry to catch up.

As he walked by, he looked up admiringly at the *Revenge* and noticed me on the bridge. I lifted my beer and nodded. He nodded in return and kept walking a couple more steps before stopping, turning back and glancing up at the small Marine Corps flag flying on the short radar mast above the overhead.

"Fine boat, Marine," he said. "Rampage?"

"Yeah," I replied.

"Don't suppose you could spare one of those beers, could ya?"

He looked a little older than Jimmy, maybe twenty-four or so. Tall and lanky, with a decided Texas drawl. "I don't usually drink with strangers," I said.

"Ken Wood, Tenth Marines," he said.

I stood up slowly and looked down at him. "Gun Bunny?"

"FDC," he replied, meaning he was with Fire Direction Control in an artillery unit. I wish I had a nickel for every poser that claimed he was Marine Recon, an Army Ranger, or Navy SEAL.

"Come aboard," I said. "Won't your ladies miss you?"

"Employers," he corrected as he set his bag on the dock and stepped lightly over the gunwale into the cockpit.

"Come on up, Wood. Name's McDermitt. Jesse McDermitt."

He climbed up the ladder to the bridge and offered his hand. He had a firm grip, without testing mine, sandy blonde hair a little over his ears and clear blue eyes. Up close, I could see that he might be a couple of years older. I handed him the last beer from the cooler. "Those two are your employers?"

I also look younger than my thirty-eight years from a distance and he must have noticed. "Yes, sir. They hired me to pilot their boat from Beaufort to Key West. They're sisters. Sounded like a pretty good gig at the time."

"Just McDermitt," I said. "Or Jesse. I'm just a retired enlisted man. Let me guess, you've been stopping three times a day so they could shop?"

"Pretty much," he replied with a chuckle. "Was supposed to be a four-day run, but it's already been eight. They paid me extra, and to be honest, the eye candy doesn't hurt, but I need to be gettin' home. When did you fall out?"

"Three months ago, from Lejeune."

"Ground pounder?"

"Sometimes. You been out long?"

"Discharged in '93, shipped over in '94 and got out again about two years ago. Downsizing."

"Desert Storm?" I asked.

"Yeah. You?"

"Force Recon, north of Al Wafra."

"Romeo, Five-Ten, Al Batin. Wait, did you say Al Wafra? Kuwait?"

"Spent most of my time there with a buddy in a spider hole, north of the city. Then another one just outside Kuwait City Airport." He gave me a puzzled look then a light went on behind his eyes.

"You're a sniper?"

"Nope, not anymore. Charter captain, now."

And just like that, as it happens to military people all the time, we found a common bond. Sand and black, burning oil smoke. We talked a while longer then he had to go get a shower so he could take the sisters back out to the boat. He pointed out a sleek looking forty foot Riviera aft cabin motor yacht moored to a buoy not far from the dinghy dock.

With nothing going on the next day, I went down and grabbed a couple more beers from the galley and returned to my perch on the bridge. I'd begun calling this late night entertainment *Dockside Follies*. The occasional inebriated transient liveaboard could be pretty comical getting into his dinghy. More than one had taken a spill.

Twenty minutes later, the door to the deck area of the bar flew open and Wood came tumbling out. Two guys shouted something from the open doorway and it closed. He got up, picked up his bag, and at first seemed like he was going to go back inside. Then he must have thought better of it and started down the dock.

I climbed down from the bridge and stood at the transom as he walked up. "What was that about?" I asked.

"Just a misunderstanding," he muttered in reply.

He explained that his employers had been drinking since earlier in the day and were pretty toasted. After he'd showered, he found them at a table with four rough looking guys and suggested they go back to the boat. One of the sisters started to get up and the guy next to her had pulled her into his lap, while two others 'escorted' him out the door.

"You think your employers might be in some trouble?" I asked.

"If they are, there ain't much I can do about it, McDermitt. Besides, both were giggling and laughing when those guys tossed me out. I'm about ready to just wash my hands of them and catch the next bus north."

"About to?"

"Naw, I guess not. Just burns me they were laughing." I could see the tenseness in his face and eyes and knew what he was about to do.

"That was just the booze. Care for a little company when you go back in?" He looked across the transom at me, trying to judge my motivation. "Come on, I'm bored sitting up there."

I vaulted the transom and landed lightly on the dock next to him. Truth was, I was pretty sure I'd seen the four men he mentioned, when they arrived an hour earlier. They weren't locals.

Wood set his bag on the dock and followed after me. "You don't have a truck in this, McDermitt."

"Maybe, maybe not. I saw the four guys earlier. They're not from around here."

I pulled open both doors and stepped inside. It was nearly closing time and there were only a handful of people still inside. Aaron and the flirtatious bartender, Robin, were just coming out of his office. She pointed toward the corner where the four men and two women sat and Aaron started that way. Wood and I started that way, too. When I caught Aaron's eye I held up my hand motioning him to wait. They never really have need of a bouncer at *Dockside*, it's more of a restaurant café than a bar and when one of the locals gets too rowdy, others are there to handle it. Besides, Aaron was barely big enough to politely ask someone to leave.

As we approached the group, both women were in two of the men's laps and it looked like they'd recently figured out they were in a bad situation and were trying to extricate themselves. The two guys on the other side of the table saw me and Wood approaching and stood up, one of them knocking his chair to the floor. Both men were rough looking.

The bigger of the two standing was only a little shorter than my six-three and heavier, but it was all flab. He had a crooked nose and mustache that said he'd taken at least one hard right hand.

The other guy was shorter and probably didn't tip the scales at more than a buck fifty. He wore his hair long, touching his shoulders and had the beginnings of a beard on his chin, even though he looked to be in his early thirties.

"I thought I told you to get lost!" Crooked Nose bellowed as he moved clumsily around the side of the table. The smaller man took a step back and to the side, his eyes darting all over the barroom and his whole body seemed to be jerking and twitching.

Great, I thought, *a meth head and he's tweaking.*

The two guys holding the women both looked back over their shoulders at me and Wood then almost simultaneously dumped them on the floor and stood up. The women scrambled away and came to their feet, moving off toward the bar unsteadily.

These two guys were big. One was my height, maybe a little more and had at one time been a powerful man, but he'd let it go to booze and drugs and it settled around his middle. He was still well past my two hundred-thirty pounds, probably two-fifty or more. He had a shaved head and the attitude that a lot of big men have, that they can push anyone around. Trouble with that is, they rarely run into anyone that pushes back, so they lack any kind of fighting skill. The other was about six feet tall and also looked like he'd passed his peak, physically, but still had a handsome face.

Baldy and Handsome stepped apart as Crooked Nose moved to Baldy's right. Tweaker remained in the corner, his eyes darting around seeing everything and nothing. Meth heads are really hard to figure. You just never know what they're going to do and rarely do what you'd expect. I took all four of them in and calculated him to be the most dangerous.

I've been in a bar fight or two. Okay, a few dozen, maybe. I wasn't sure about Wood, though. Would he run, or would he stand. He looked steady enough and being a Texican, he'd probably been in a few fights himself. As if reading my mind, Wood said forcefully, "We're leaving. All four of us."

"Ya got that wrong, kid," Baldy growled. "You two are leavin' and these two are leavin' with us."

The challenge was plain, the gauntlet laid down. The first to speak is always the leader. Take out the leader and the others usually cave. So that's exactly what I did. The rum stink of Baldy's words had barely left his mouth when I shifted the weight to my left foot, turned slightly, and executed a snap side kick that caught him flush in the face, lifting him completely off the deck and depositing him spread eagle on the table, out cold. The table swayed slightly for a second and then seemed to vibrate and collapse under his weight.

I turned to Handsome, but kept Tweaker in my peripheral vision. "You really have only one choice here," I said. "You're leaving. The matter of how you do it is up to you. Carrying Baldy or being carried by the EMTs. Make your choice."

Tweaker made it for him, charging at Wood and grabbing a chair. Crooked Nose moved quickly to his right, trying to flank me. I held my arms wide, palms up, as if saying, 'This is how you want it' and took a slight step toward Handsome, drawing Crooked Nose further to my left flank and slightly behind me.

I timed it just about right, clapping both hands as hard as I could on the side of Handsome's face. I knew the force would rupture one or both ear drums, an extremely painful experience. Crooked Nose came at me from behind, as I knew he would. I spun completely around to my right, bringing my elbow smashing into the side of his head. He nearly did a cartwheel as he went down next to Baldy, on top of what was left of the table. Handsome had fallen to his knees, both hands cupping the sides of his head screaming in pain, with blood trickling between his fingers. If the tables were reversed, I doubted these men would show quarter, so I didn't. I stepped forward and brought my right knee straight into his face. He landed in a heap on top of his two friends.

I heard a crash and turned to my right. The chair Tweaker had grabbed disintegrated across Wood's back and shoulder as he stepped into the blow. In a heartbeat, he was upright and took the little man into a suplex move that I'd only seen on late night wrestling TV shows. Tweaker landed hard across Baldy's legs, his head snapping back onto the floor, knocking him out cold.

"Guess it's the EMTs, then," I hissed. I turned to the two women. "You better go with your Captain, now." They rushed past me toward Wood, almost stumbling over the pile of men and table parts on the floor. Turning to Wood I said, "Go. The cops'll be here any minute. I'll take care of this."

The three hurried out the door as I reached into my pocket for my money clip. I quickly peeled off two hundreds and stepped over to the bar where Aaron and Robin still stood. Stuffing the two bills into the tip jar I said, "Sorry, Aaron. That'll cover the table and chair." Pointing to the four men, I added, "Those four beat each other up, right?"

"Huh," he said a little in shock. "Um, yeah. That's what happened. Go. I got it covered."

As I trotted out the back door, I could hear sirens approaching the front and saw Wood and the two women rowing away from the dock, both women chattering animatedly. He lifted his head in salute as he bent into the oars and yelled, "Semper Fi, McDermitt."

I waved at him as I stepped aboard the *Revenge*, still shaking a little from the adrenaline rush. I went into the salon and poured a couple fingers of Myers's Rum and tossed it down, feeling the burn in the back of my throat. A few dozen and one. But, who's counting.

CHAPTER FIVE

I t was well past sunrise and I was sitting on the bridge enjoying a cup of coffee and listening to the marina sounds. Gulls wheeling and diving for breakfast, the bell like ring of steel cables on aluminum masts, and the occasional splash of baitfish trying to fly away from an unseen predator below.

I heard a sound and turned to see Wood and one of the women bumping the dinghy dock. He tied off and the two of them climbed out and walked over. "Permission to come aboard?" Wood asked.

"Welcome," I replied then grinned and added, "I'm all out of beer, though."

He laughed, as I climbed down the ladder to the cockpit and shook his hand. "Captain McDermitt, this is Miss Charlotte Richmond, of Beaufort. Miss Richmond, Captain Jesse McDermitt."

"Pleased to meet you, Captain," she said with a charming southern drawl while offering her hand, which I took. She had a firm dry grip. "Or may I call you Jesse?"

"Any way you choose, Miss Richmond."

She was even more striking in the soft morning daylight. About five feet, eight inches tall, a nice figure, brown wavy hair past her shoulders, with a touch of highlighter maybe, and ivory skin, which just didn't work down here. She looked to be around thirty, but her eyes were a little cloudy, maybe from drinking too much the day before.

"Please call me Sharlee, all my friends do."

"I was just about to go into the galley for some coffee," I said. "Would y'all care to join me?"

"Thank you," she replied. "We'd love to."

I opened the hatch to the salon and followed them inside. "Have a seat anywhere."

She took a seat in the middle of the l-shaped sofa to port and Wood took the narrower part of the sofa aft. I've met women like Miss Richmond from Beaufort before. Everything they do, even choosing a place to sit, is intentional. I poured coffee in three mugs, set them on a small folding table that is stored by the freezer, along with a sugar bowl and cream dispenser and carried it around the island to the salon. Her choice of seating left only enough room to sit close to her, so I leaned against the island and watched her over the rim of my mug, taking a drink.

"Your boat is beautiful, Jesse," she said. "I never dreamed a fishing boat would be so luxurious."

"Thanks. Is there something I can do for y'all?"

She took a sip from the coffee, looking back at me with big brown eyes. "I just wanted to say thank you," she said. "For what you did last night. I'm afraid my sister, Savannah, and I might have had a little too much to drink."

"Wait," I said. "Charlotte and Savannah Richmond, from Beaufort?"

"We get that a lot. Daddy's name is Jackson and Momma's is Madison. They felt it necessary to continue the tradition."

"Got a brother named Memphis, by any chance?"

She laughed and said that no, they didn't have any brothers.

"So, where's your sister?" I asked.

"I'm afraid Savannah doesn't share my sense of etiquette. Don't get me wrong, Jesse. I love my sister, but at times she can be quite a handful."

"Don't give last night another thought, Miss Richmond," I said. Her eyes told me she would have preferred my using her first name. Her manner told me she preferred having things her own way and was used to it.

"Just helping a fellow Marine out of a bad situation. But, if you don't mind a little friendly advice, it would probably be a wise decision on you and your sister's parts, to heed your Captain's warnings. While this area might seem quiet and serene, these are pirate waters. Always have been. Had it not been for him, the two of you might have been sold as sex slaves this morning and your boat used in drug trafficking this afternoon." That caused her cheeks to redden a bit.

She placed the coffee mug on the saucer and stood up. "Thank you for your hospitality, Captain. But, we really must be going now."

Wood stood up and gave me a slight eye roll as she headed toward the hatch. I shook Wood's hand as I opened the hatch for her and she strode out onto the deck. "Be careful," I warned him. "There really are pirates in these waters."

"Thanks, Gunny."

Once they left, I put away the table and washed the dishes, before pouring another cup of coffee and heading back out to the cockpit. Deciding I'd had enough of sitting on the bridge, I opened the hatch to the engine room and stepped down. Flicking on the light, I got a pleasant surprise. Jimmy must have scrubbed and polished everything in sight. The engines, generator, compressor, and everything else were gleaming like new. I went ahead and checked the oil and filters in everything and cleaned out the water intake filters, though there was very little debris.

As I was coming up the ladder, a woman's voice called out, "Where can I find the Captain?" It was the sister, Savannah.

"I'm Captain McDermitt," I said. "What can I do for you?"

"You were rude to my sister, bud."

Bud? I thought. *Charlotte did say she was a handful, but bud?*

I climbed up the last two steps and walked over to the transom where she stood on the dock, hands on her hips. If anything, she was more beautiful than her sister. Taller, about five-ten, a couple of years older, but it was hard to tell. She was dark tanned, blonde hair streaked by the sun, and had the body of an athlete.

"How was I rude?" I asked.

"That story about being sold as a slave."

"Sex slave," I corrected her, placing my empty mug on the transom. "And it isn't a story. Happens all the time in the Caribbean. Just a week ago the seventeen and fifteen-year-old daughters of a couple were abducted along with the mother. They were cruising ten miles south of Boca Chica. The father was shot, but lived to tell the tale. The girls and their mother still haven't been found. Probably in some Saudi sheik's harem, by now."

No color came to this woman's cheeks. "Stay away from my sister, if you know what's good for you."

"She's not my type," I shouted as she stomped off toward the dinghy dock in her bare feet and cutoff jeans. Just then Jimmy came down the dock from the opposite direction.

Both of us watched her retreating form and having heard my shout, Jimmy said, "I'm thinking that one might be, dude. What was that all about?"

"Just a couple of tourist women," I said. "Charlotte and Savannah Richmond, of the Beaufort Richmonds," I added with a southern drawl. "Hey, I was just down in the engine room. Looks like you could eat off the deck down there."

"Just doing my job, el Capitan. What's on for today?"

"We got nothing on the schedule," I said. "You have any plans?"

"Nada, man."

"Then let's go to an electronics store. You can help me pick out a good sound system."

"I know just the guy, man." I figured he would.

After setting the alarm and locking up, I vaulted over the transom. As we walked toward the parking lot, I glanced back and saw Savannah rowing the little dinghy like it was a crewing shell. Her wide shoulders and long, tanned arms pulling for the finish line. Just a little more speed and she'd have it up on plane.

As I headed toward my old International, Jimmy said, "It's only half a mile, man."

So we walked up Sombrero Boulevard to a place near US-1 called Sea Wiz Marine Systems. I'd noticed the shop before but hadn't needed anything to this point.

We spent the next hour talking to the owner about a stereo system and he asked a lot of questions about my boat and musical tastes. They had a wide variety of stereo systems, amplifiers, and speakers made specifically for boats. They also carried a good assortment of wind and solar generator systems. With the owner's and Jimmy's help we picked out what we wanted, including some backup systems for electrical power. The owner said they weren't busy and he could have two of his technicians at the dock in an hour and have it all installed and working by the afternoon.

"What kind of radar and fish finder do you have aboard?" the guy asked. "We don't sell much in that line, but I have a friend that does."

I described the systems aboard and he said, "Sounds like good equipment. If you want, I could have my friend stop by and take a look. Maybe offer some suggestions." Jimmy agreed that the systems we had aboard were probably adequate, but it wouldn't hurt to hear what's new, since electronics were obsolete as soon as they hit the store.

Just before noon, a Sea Wiz van pulled up in the parking lot and two men got out. Another white van pulled up next to the first about the same time and a third man got out and all three came over to the dock.

The three men introduced themselves and I invited them aboard. The two guys from Sea Wiz went straight to work and the other man, Ken, climbed up to the bridge with me.

After examining the radar and fish finders he turned to me and said, "Your mate was right. This is all good equipment. Top of the line, in fact. Ever think of adding forward and side scan sonar?"

"What for?" I asked sounding like a land lubber.

"Some channels are pretty narrow and could have obstructions, or turns. Finding a cut through a reef is a breeze with forward scanning sonar. Especially at night."

"You'd have to pull her out of the water?"

"No sir," he said surprising me. "I've developed my own system. I put a watertight cover over the area in the bilge I want to mount the transducer, with a sonic sending unit mounted inside and cut the hole under-water, using a sensor to find the sending unit."

"Ever missed?"

"A couple times when I was developing it. Those were just plywood on sawhorses, though. Done it to forty-four boats in the water and hit dead center every time."

"How much?"

"Installation of the transducer, wiring, installation of the receiver, all other parts and labor, I could do you up right for nine-thousand dollars."

"Can you do it up right for eight-thousand?"

He thought it over a moment. "Since Jimmy works for ya, eighty-five hundred."

"Do it," I said. "But, if you sink it, you bought it."

By mid-afternoon, all the work was done. The new sonar screen mounted in the console really set us apart from other charter boats. The stereo system consisted of a ten-CD changer, stereo, and amplifier, mounted in the entertainment center in the salon.

The speakers in the salon and staterooms were so small I was real surprised at the sound quality. Water-proof speakers were mounted in the aft bulkhead for the cockpit and four more on the bridge. Sea Wiz even threw in an intercom system, with units in both state-rooms, the galley, cockpit, and on the bridge, all wire-less. The whole day cost almost twelve grand.

Jimmy surprised me once more, when he switched on the CD player and Coltrane filled the bridge with smooth jazz. "I would have guessed you for a head banger," I said.

"Dude, please. Not that I don't like rock, too. I listen to a little of everything, but jazz is music for the soul, man."

We drank a couple of beers then Jimmy said he had a date and left. Rusty stopped by and we sat on the bridge drinking until well past sunset, while listening to a Cuban radio station. Rusty surprised me by translating what the DJ said.

"I didn't know you spoke Spanish," I said.

"I understand it more than I can talk it. It's pretty necessary down here. Wouldn't hurt you to learn a little."

We talked some more and I told him about the fight and meeting the sisters. An hour later, he said he had to get up early and left.

CHAPTER SIX

The smell of fresh coffee woke me the next morning. The coffee maker had a timer and I'd taken to setting it up before going to bed. It was better than an alarm clock. Sitting on the bridge, I watched the night sky slowly turn purple, then the first finger rays of the rising sun lit up the clouds hanging over the eastern horizon. I'd always reveled in watching the sun rise and set in different places around the world. No matter where I was, it looked the same and different at the same time.

I heard a splash and looked toward the sound. Savannah was tying up their dinghy. Just what I needed. She climbed out and walked along the dock toward the *Revenge*. Stopping at my pier she looked up and said, "I think I owe you an apology." She lifted a thermos. "Can I buy you a cup of Australian coffee?"

Never one to turn down someone else's brew, I said, "Sure, come aboard."

She sat on the transom and swung two tanned and shapely legs over, stepping down to the deck in bare feet. I climbed down and met her in the cockpit. "Come on in," I said as I held the hatch open.

She stepped up into the galley. "Wow! This is a really cool yacht. I thought it was a fishing boat."

"It is," I said. "Kind of a reverse mullet. Party up front and all business in the rear."

"You're dating yourself. Nobody wears a mullet anymore."

"Have a seat, I'll get another mug."

She slid into the settee booth and twisted the top off the thermos, unconcerned about where I'd sit. I didn't bother with a saucer, sugar, or cream and my guess was right, as she poured both our mugs with the strong smelling coffee and took a sip.

"I asked around about what you said. About the sex slave thing. I'm sorry I accused you of lying. Also, thanks for bailing us out the other night. Sharlee is a little gullible sometimes and I was way toasted."

I noticed that she didn't have a hint of southern drawl like her sister and asked her about it.

"Sharlee went to 'finishing school'," she said, rolling her eyes at the words. "I was sort of a tomboy and preferred to go out on my dad's fishing boats."

"Boats? Plural?"

"Yeah, he owns a fleet of commercial boats. I skippered one until he retired and sold the fleet."

"Really?"

She used both hands holding her mug, as she took another sip. "You like the coffee?"

I'd finished half the cup and hardly noticed it. "Yeah, it's great," I said looking into her blue eyes.

"Where'd you learn to fight like that? You went through the three biggest guys like a hot knife through butter."

"Fight? Oh, the other night. I studied a little martial arts. You and your sister are as different as night and day."

"Thanks, I love her, but she can be a handful sometimes." I nearly spit out my coffee. "What?" she asked.

As I tried to control my laughter I said, "She said almost exactly the same thing about you."

Refilling both our cups she said, "We've decided to stay here a while."

"What brought you to the Keys, anyway?"

"Mom and Dad went to Australia. That's where the coffee came from, they sent it to me. Sharlee doesn't like coffee."

"So, I guess Captain Wood will be leaving?"

"Tomorrow. He was planning to take a bus, but since we took so much longer getting down here, we bought him an airline ticket. The way he talked, it sounded like you two knew each other. Do you?"

"Not really," I said. "We chewed the same sand, served in Desert Storm. Just met the other night."

"You were a Marine, too?"

I let the 'were' slide. "Yeah, I retired a few months ago."

"You're way too young to retire."

"Which is why I'm working as a charter boat Captain."

We talked for another twenty minutes and finished the coffee when Jimmy showed up. Meeting him on the dock, Jimmy and I stood watching as she walked back to her dinghy. As he started to say something I held up a finger, watching her. At the end of the dock, she looked back over her shoulder at the two of us and waved.

"She looked back," I said waving.

"Yeah, so?"

"She didn't yesterday."

"You're losing me, dude."

I stepped over the transom and said, "If a woman looks back as she's walking away, she's interested."

"Ah, one of those body language things, huh?"

We spent an hour checking on the boat. I was still learning a lot about it and he seemed to have an un-limited supply of knowledge. I told him that on days we didn't have a charter he didn't even need to come down to the marina and if something came up, I'd call him.

I powered up my laptop and we checked emails from the website. I still wanted to keep my workdays to a minimum, so we often told prospective clients we were booked. Jimmy suggested we raise our rates.

"We're priced like every other dive operator and we only take six divers out," he said. "A lot of people would be willing to pay more for that kind of service. And dude, nothing cuts out the serious divers from the am-ateurs like money."

So, we raised our prices. We also offered a slightly lower group rate. There were four emails, requesting slots for seven dives total. All of them wanted Saturday. I suggested to Jimmy that we only work weekdays and he seemed to like that. It would further cut our clientele by weeding out the weekend warriors. Just as I was about to shut the thing off, another email came in. It was from a friend of one of the photographers we took out a few days earlier. He wanted to book the boat for a whole night, any night this week, for just three dive photographers. They wanted to dive in the twenty to forty foot range starting at dusk.

"All night?" Jimmy said.

"What's the going rate around here for something like that?" I asked.

"Got me, man. Nobody does it."

"Send him a reply. Tell him the rate's ten percent higher than an all-day charter, make it thirteen-hundred."

"We don't do all day charters, dude."

"He doesn't know that."

Jimmy sent the reply, dressing it up to include free tank refills, photo editing, and breakfast at *Dockside*. The reply came back almost immediately, asking what nights were available.

"Damn," I said. "He bit."

"We'll need a third hand on board, man. Someone to help out refilling tanks and piloting, while I'm working with the photography."

"Tell him tomorrow night, I have someone in mind."

He sent the message and got a reply back immediately again, booking it. The guy said he'd stop by later in the afternoon and give me a deposit.

"Wow, dude," Jimmy said. "That's almost double what anyone else charges and he didn't hesitate. Who you got in mind to help out? Rusty?"

"I'll ask around," I said glancing out the starboard porthole. "Why don't you take off? Get to bed early this evening and meet me here at zero-three-hundred. We can get everything ready by eleven-hundred and get a few hours of sleep on board in the afternoon."

After he left, I went up to the bridge with a cooler of beer. The Richmond sisters and Wood were rowing toward the dinghy dock. Once they tied off and started toward *Dockside*, I stood at the rail and lifted my beer. "Got a minute, Captain?"

Charlotte kept walking, her nose in the air, as I'd hoped she would. Savannah and Wood stopped at the transom and Wood said, "Catching a flight in about an hour, but that's plenty of time for a beer I guess."

"What about you, Savannah?" I asked. "Have a beer with a couple of boat bums?"

"Boat bums are my favorite people to drink with," she said then turned to her sister and called out, "I'll catch up in a minute, Sharlee."

The woman never broke stride, just waved over her shoulder and kept going. Wood vaulted over the transom and offered his hand to Savannah, who ignored it and stepped lightly to the deck in her bare feet. I wondered if she ever wore shoes.

"Come on up," I said. I switched on the stereo, turned very low and clicked the CD changer's remote switch a few times. The sound of John McLaughlin's double neck guitar started to quietly fill the bridge, as if from nowhere.

Wood noticed the new sonar screen and said, "That's way cool, Gunny. Sonar?"

"Just installed, it can scan forward, backward, and to the sides. Should make picking my way through holes in the reef a lot easier. Have a seat." I offered them both a bottle of Kalik and they accepted.

"What's a gunny?" Savannah asked.

"It was my rank, before I retired," I said. "Just wanted to have a farewell drink, Wood. Savannah said you were flying out."

"I appreciate the hospitality," he said. "It's always good meeting a fellow Jarhead."

I extended my bottle and he clinked the neck of his to it.

"Is that Mahavishnu?" Savannah asked.

"Now look who's dating themselves," I said. "How is it that you know McLaughlin?"

"He still tours. I caught him in Munich last summer."

Turning back to Wood, I said, "I also wanted to ask if you'd consider delaying your departure, Wood? I just had a short-term job open up."

"What kind of job?"

"I have an all-night dive charter tomorrow night that came up suddenly, a group of photographers. My first mate will be busy between dives helping them edit their pictures and videos. I could use someone to help pilot the boat, while I hook up the air compressor to refill the tanks for the next dive. Depart before dusk and back by sunrise."

"Wish I could help you out, but I've already been gone longer than I figured on."

I looked over at Savannah and said, "You're a licensed skipper, right?"

She thought about it for a second and said, "Sure I can help you out. Hanging around with Sharlee all night can get a bit tedious anyway."

Wood had a flight to catch, so they left soon after to collect Charlotte at *Dockside*. I noticed the three of them leave a few minutes later and get into a red convertible, obviously a rental, with Savannah behind the wheel.

Thirty minutes later, the red convertible pulled back into the parking lot with only Savannah in it. She got out and went inside, emerging five minutes later. As she walked toward the dinghy dock I called down, "What happened to your sister?"

"Got any more beer?" she asked.

I invited her up to the bridge, where she told me that Charlotte had booked a flight at the last minute for San Francisco. So she'd rented a slip and would be staying awhile.

"She booked a flight to Frisco without any baggage?"

"She'll just buy whatever she needs when she gets there. It's not the first time she's done this."

We talked for a few minutes longer. I asked her to be here at eighteen-hundred, rested, and ready to go. The clients would arrive at nineteen-hundred. She left after that, to move her boat to a slip three down from mine. I offered to help, but she declined. "Like I said, Sharlee's ditched me more than once, leaving me to single hand the boat."

I watched from the bridge as she got the dinghy aboard and started the engines on the big Riviera. Letting them warm up, she went forward and checked the line securing the boat to the mooring ball, checked the current in the bay and looked aft where several boats were moored behind her. She made a decision and went back to the helm. She put it in gear then scrambled forward to untie the line as the boat slowly idled forward against the current.

In an instant she had cast off the mooring line and was back at the helm, expertly maneuvering the big luxury yacht toward the dock, swinging it around to back in. A few minutes later, she had her backed in, tied off, and shut down the engines. I was impressed.

CHAPTER SEVEN

The following day, I woke at zero-two-thirty and had coffee on the bridge. Jimmy arrived right on time and we spent the next several hours cleaning, polishing, and getting the equipment ready. After that, we spent some time checking tides and dive sites. We chose five shallow reefs that aren't visited by dive charter boats very often. By staying on shallow reefs the divers could make multiple dives, without worrying much about nitrogen buildup. Before noon, we turned in to get some sleep before the clients arrived.

The smell of coffee woke me at seventeen-thirty. I poured a cup and went up to the bridge. A few minutes later, Jimmy joined me. "Did you ever find someone to help us out?" he asked, watching Savannah walk toward us with a bag over her shoulder. She was dressed in jeans and a man's work shirt, but had the tails tied at her belly, showing off an inch or two of tanned skin.

"Sure did," I said.

"Permission to board, Captain," Savannah asked from the dock.

"Stow your gear in the hanging closet just inside the hatch," I told her. "There's coffee in the galley. Mugs are right above it."

"She's our crew?" Jimmy asked. His mouth hung open, watching her sit on the transom and swing her legs over. She was barefoot again.

When she joined us on the bridge, I introduced them and said, "Savannah's going to be a neighbor for a while."

Less than an hour later the clients arrived, two men and a young woman, all carrying dive bags and hard cases that I assumed contained expensive camera equipment. While I started the engines, Jimmy and Savannah helped them stow their gear in the salon and Jimmy showed them around the boat.

They made a total of six dives and everything went very well. Savannah handled the boat whenever we had to move between dives, using the GPS and waypoints I'd already entered. That allowed me to swap tanks for the divers, while they worked in the salon with Jimmy. They made two dives on one of the reefs we'd chosen and one dive on the other four.

We were back at the dock just as the sun was beginning to turn the eastern sky purple and I treated the clients to breakfast at *Dockside*. Jimmy's ability with both the still and video editing software was a huge hit. He wired the laptop to the high definition flat screen TV in the salon, so the divers could see much larger images and video clips. After breakfast, all three divers tipped Jimmy and Savannah a hundred dollars each and promised to feature our operation on their website.

With an extra three bills in his pocket, Jimmy took off shortly after the clients left. "He has a lot of talent," Savannah said over coffee. "And you seem to have carved quite a niche among the underwater photography community."

"Actually, that was a first," I said. "They were referred by another group we took out a few days ago. Not sure if I want to do a lot of overnight charters, though."

"Well, it was fun," she said. "But, I've got to get some sleep." She got up from the table and started toward the door, where she stopped and looked back over her shoulder.

"See ya later," I said as she waved.

Jimmy and I had two more very successful charters that week, one of which was a direct result of the photographers mention on their website. Savannah helped out once again with that charter. She said she just enjoyed being out on the water and would be glad to help out whenever she could. When I broached the subject of going out on a date Saturday, she shot me down in flames.

"Nothing personal," she said. "You're a sweet guy and good looking as all get out. But, I just got through a pretty nasty divorce a few weeks ago. This trip with Sharlee was supposed to be my celebration." I didn't push it anymore but did enjoy having her around and although it wasn't a date, we sat on the bridge Saturday evening, drank a few beers and watched the sun go down.

We had another hurricane scare the following week, Tropical Storm Harvey. When I heard about it on the NOAA weather radio, it had just formed in the Gulf, about three hundred miles west of the Keys and was headed north-northeast, away from us. That night it turned easterly and early the next day, it was headed straight toward Marathon.

A few boat owners began making ready to bug out by afternoon. I went over to the *Anchor* and everything seemed normal. Rusty and Julie weren't making any preparations at all. I found Rusty out by the shallow canal, his back to me. As I walked up behind him, without turning he said, "Feels the same as that day with Floyd, don't it, Jesse."

I stepped up beside him and closed my eyes. He was right, the air felt heavier and I could hear the small waves on the shoreline more than a hundred yards away. "Yeah," I said. "It'll turn east, won't it?"

When I opened my eyes he was looking at me. "But ya had to come by to make sure?"

"I still have much to learn, Master," I said with an overly dramatic bow.

"One day," he said looking out over the canal, "I think I might dredge this canal and make the basin wider. Only boats that can get up here are flats skiffs."

We went back inside. Julie was out shopping and Rufus was behind the bar. I hadn't had the chance yet to meet him, being busy with the charter business.

"You must be Rufus," I said sitting down on a stool at the end.

"Ya sir," he said with less of an accent than I would have thought, with his Jamaican heritage. "You muss be Cap'n McDermitt."

"I am. How'd you know?"

"It a beanie island, sir. Word get aroun." Turning to Rusty he said, "Anders jest left. He drop off some fresh hogfish. Yuh two want a sandwich?"

"Hogfish?" Rufus nodded. "Absolutely, mon!" Turning to me Rusty said, "You're in for a real treat."

"I've had hogfish before, Rusty."

"Not like this, you ain't," he said as Rufus headed out the back door. "Rufus just had some seasonings sent over from his cousin in Jamaica. Wait till you taste this."

We had coffee while we waited. The smell coming from the grill out back was making me very hungry. Rusty was right, the things Rufus could do with some simple seasonings were out of this world.

CHAPTER EIGHT

Over the next few weeks, Jimmy and I became inundated with requests for dive charters and had to turn several away. Jimmy went online and found not just one, but three websites promoting stories about our operation featuring some terrific underwater photos and highlighting his photo editing abilities. We had to turn quite a few down.

Early on a Wednesday in mid-October another hurricane scare became a reality. Tropical Storm Irene formed off the western tip of the Yucatan and started moving north, threatening western Cuba.

I heard Rusty's voice from the dock, as I stared at the constantly changing weather radar on the Weather Channel. "Ahoy *Revenge*."

I stepped out into the cockpit where a light rain was falling and invited my old friend aboard. Jimmy was just a few steps behind, even though it was more than an hour before sunrise. I noticed there was a lot more activity in the marina than was normal for this hour.

"What's your plan?" Rusty asked.

"I've decided on a forty-eight hour window," I replied as Jimmy stepped aboard.

"We're only a couple hours from that, Skipper," Jimmy said.

"He's right. It won't be much of a blow, but when it crosses Cuba and gets into the warm waters of the Strait, it'll become a hurricane. No telling how strong it'll get crossing the Straits, but it is going to hit here."

Savannah came down the dock wearing cutoff jeans and a yellow rain slicker, bare feet as usual. She stood listening. "Will it be safe here in the harbor?" she asked.

"Probably," Rusty replied. "At least here at the docks. All those boats out there on the hook is a different story."

She looked across the harbor at the thirty or so boats tied with a single line to mooring buoys. "What if one of them breaks loose?"

"More than one will. Seen it happen quite a few times," Jimmy said then turned to me. "We taking her out?"

I made my decision then and there, not willing to take the risk of a boat, adrift in high winds, slamming into my bow. "We'll leave just after first light."

"You're going to go out in this rain?" Savannah asked.

"We're heading north to Shark River," I said. "It's safer there."

She only thought about it a second and asked, "Mind if I follow along?"

"Single handed? It could get pretty rough."

"I'll go with her," Rusty said. "Won't take me more than thirty minutes to prep the bar. Rufus has been through a hundred of these, he'll manage fine without me."

"What about Julie?" I asked.

"She went up to Homestead last night. Not planning to be back for a couple of days."

Together, we went over to the *Anchor* and helped Rusty get things ready. There really wasn't a lot to do, he didn't have much outside and only needed to trailer his skiff and anchor it between two trees in the yard. He had corrugated metal covers for all the windows, with anchor bolts set in the framework around each one. Within minutes, we had them all up and Rufus's little shack buttoned up against the impending storm. Rusty brought a chainsaw out and said, "Never know when you might need to cut a tree out of the way."

Back at the docks, Rusty and Jimmy prepared to cast off the lines, while Savannah and I got our engines started. I keyed the VHF mic and said, "Are you on sixteen, Savannah?"

"Roger, Jesse," came her reply.

"Go to sixty-nine." I switched frequencies and waited a moment. "What's your top speed?"

"If it's calm, I can make about twenty-five knots. You?"

"A bit more," I said. "Y'all take the lead, when we get into the Bay we'll spread out a little."

"Are you sure about all this?"

"Rusty's lived here all his life and his family's been here for over a hundred years. If he says Tarpon Bay is the place to go, I'll take his word on it."

A few minutes later, we passed the old Highway 931 bridge, now just a fishing pier, and into open water. The seas were pretty choppy with no apparent wave direction and the wind was blowing a steady twenty-five knots or so, out of the east, driving the rain under the top, into the bridge. Savannah's Riviera had a fully enclosed aft deck and bridge, so they were at least staying dry. I noticed the name on the stern for the first time, *Savannah Daydreamin'*.

"She must be a Buffett fan," Jimmy said noticing it too.

"Buffett? I don't get it."

"From his album, *Havana Daydreamin'*," he explained. "He has a daughter named Savannah Jane. A play on words."

I followed behind her for the next thirty minutes as Rusty guided her around Pigeon Key Banks, under the Seven Mile Bridge, through East Bahia Honda Channel, and into Florida Bay. Once we cleared Bluefish and Monkey Banks, I accelerated and came alongside her, about a hundred feet off her port side.

It was a little calmer in the Gulf and we made good time, but it was still an hour before we reached the other side and Ponce De Leon Bay, where Shark River flows into the Gulf of Mexico. We came down off plane and started up the river, behind another yacht.

It seems Rusty's hurricane hole wasn't much of a secret to the cruising crowd.

"*Revenge* go to twenty-four," Rusty's voice came over the VHF speaker.

I changed frequencies and said, "Go ahead, Rusty."

"It'll take us about two hours to make Tarpon Bay. We'll stick to the river, instead of the canal and enter the bay on the west side. There's a cove just north of there that's wide enough to lash the boats together and is sheltered on three sides by tall mangroves."

"Lead the way, brother."

Another voice came over the speaker, "This is *M/V Osprey*. Sorry to listen in. Are you the two yachts behind us?"

"Ten four, *Osprey*," Rusty replied. "*Savannah Daydreamin'* on your stern and *Gaspar's Revenge* behind us."

"We're heading to Tarpon Bay, also. I have my wife and daughters aboard. Is that cove you mentioned large enough for three?"

"What's your draft, *Osprey*."

"We're a thirty-four foot Mainship, with a three-foot-eight draft," he replied.

"What do you think, Jesse? The cove's wide enough. You have the deepest draft."

I keyed the mic and said, "Let's do it."

"*Osprey*," Rusty said, "You and I will hold off while the *Revenge* anchors and ties off to stern. He has much better ground tackle than either of us. Then we can tie off to his port and starboard and get lines out to the trees."

"Thank you, *Savannah Daydreamin'*. The name's Alexander. Josh Alexander. We were caught flatfooted and have never weathered a hurricane afloat."

"Glad to help, Josh. I'm Rusty Thurman and Jesse McDermitt is aboard the *Revenge*."

When we finally got to Tarpon Bay, the wind was a bit stronger and there were white caps on the bay itself. The cove Rusty mentioned was much calmer and surrounded by tall, stately mangrove trees that have very deep roots.

The cove was actually the mouth of a shallow creek and was a good six feet deep. Jimmy tied an orange float ball to the anchor with ten feet of line, before dropping the heavy Danforth a good hundred yards from where we wanted to tie up. The ball would allow the other two to stay clear of my anchor chain and warn anyone else coming into the bay that the cove was taken. Using the sonar pointing aft, I slowly backed toward the narrow part of the creek. When I was still thirty feet from a spot we wanted to tie off, I disengaged the clutch on the windlass and added more power to the engines to get a good bite on the bottom.

Jimmy had the little inflatable Zodiac ready and took two lines toward the trees astern of us. Landing in this part of the Everglades isn't permitted, so rather than go ashore and pull the lines tight, he simply tied off near the roots of two healthy, massive mangroves and came back, while I held position at anchor. Within minutes he had both lines tied off to the stern cleats and I called Rusty on the radio to back in.

Rusty and Savannah did the same, dropping her largest anchor near mine and backing in. Rusty had her fenders off on the port side and she slowly maneuvered back, setting the anchor and then easing over to my rail.

Jimmy remained on the dinghy and took more lines to more trees on her starboard side, as the *Osprey* began maneuvering back on my port side. By the time Josh was anchored and tied off to me, Jimmy had returned to *Daydreamin'* with the lines. Then he motored around to the *Osprey* where he took their lines and carried them toward the opposite shore and tied off.

We had three anchors, four lines to each side and four more to the stern of our raft. Josh introduced his wife Tonia and their two teenage daughters, Angela and Vanessa.

"We don't have enough lines out," Rusty said. "Let's put another dink in the water and add a dozen more. Everyone else should get to work removing canvas and stowing anything that's not part of the deck inside."

Working together, we had all three boats as storm ready as Rusty thought necessary just before nightfall. As we all headed into the salon on the *Revenge* to escape the mosquitoes and decide what to do the next day, I noticed an ugly, old converted shrimp boat come into the bay from the river. At first it headed straight toward our anchorage then stopped in the middle of the bay, about a quarter mile away, before turning and motoring further east to a smaller cove.

Once inside the salon, I took a spare set of binoculars from the hanging closet next to the hatch and looked out the portside porthole and watched as the slow moving trawler passed by. I couldn't see clearly through the rain streaked glass, but at one point a man stepped out of the pilot house. It was the bald guy from *Dockside*. The big guy whose nose I'd smashed with a well-timed side kick.

"What's wrong?" Rusty asked, standing next to me watching the old trawler.

"Remember that fight at *Dockside* I told you about a few days back. One of the guys is on that boat."

"Everybody has to be somewhere, bro."

"Yeah, not much we can do about it, I guess."

Rusty turned to the others and said, "Folks, we're gonna be here at least two days, maybe longer. There's no cell service out here and the nearest TV is probably beyond reception range."

"That ain't a problem, dude," Jimmy said. "I have a satellite internet account and Jesse has a laptop. Give me ten minutes and I can connect the big screen to his laptop, sign on, and we can get weather updates and watch internet movies."

"You can do that?" I asked.

"Sure, man." He lifted a bag out of the hanging closet and added, "I should have everything I need in here." He went over to the settee, where the Alexander's kids were sitting and started pulling out all kinds of bundled cables. Handing a CD to the oldest girl, he directed her on how to install the software and connect to the satellite service.

"Even if this storm makes a direct hit here, we'll be safe," Rusty said. "Much safer than at *Dockside*. These mangroves have a root system like no other tree on earth. The roots can run laterally underground for hundreds of feet and sink deeper roots all along the length of the main roots. With three boats rafted together, we'll be a lot more stable, too. Best of all, there's no coconut palms around here."

"Why's that good?" Tonia asked.

"Well, a coconut falling on your head ain't no good," Rusty said with a chuckle. "Imagine one being blown through the air at a hundred miles an hour."

"I got the signal," Angela said and tapped a few keys. "Here's the Weather Channel radar," she added, turning the laptop around so everyone could see. As we all crowded around it, the image suddenly appeared on the big screen TV above the settee.

I nodded at my first mate. "Good job, Jimmy."

The image on the radar loop kept moving steadily northward, heading straight for Isle of Youth, a large island south of and owned by Cuba. Then the image would jump back and loop again.

"Can you pull up an updated prediction of where it's going?" Savannah asked.

Jimmy turned the laptop toward him and worked quickly at the keyboard. A moment later, we were watching the Weather Channel's latest hurricane update, showing a predicted path that would cross Cuba, possibly intensify in the warm water of the Florida Straits, and was forecasted to turn northwest into the Gulf.

Rusty frowned as he studied the weather map, "I don't think that's what it's gonna do."

"You want to elaborate on that?" I asked.

"It'll turn northwest, sure," he said. "But, once it gets into the Straits, it's gonna turn northeast. Might miss Florida altogether, but my guess is, it'll turn a little north of northeast."

Getting a chart of the western Caribbean from the chart locker, I rolled it out on the table. "This is the Isle of Youth, where they predict it'll make landfall," I told the group, pointing at the chart. "If Rusty's right, and it turns a little northwest here, then northeast when it gets to the Straits, it'll either pass the southern tip of the state, or cross the upper or middle Keys into the Gulf. That'll put it on a straight course for where we are."

"Yeah, man," Jimmy said. "But, it won't get here until at least Friday afternoon. So, we got almost two whole days to get completely ready."

We prepared supper and everyone ate aboard the *Revenge*, while we made plans for the worsening storm. Later, after the sun had gone down, I occasionally heard music wafting from the old trawler. It seemed they were having a hurricane party.

Josh and his family retired to their boat early. I suggested that if Savannah had room, that Rusty should bunk aboard with her. The four of us set up a two and a half hour watch schedule, Jimmy took the first, then me, Rusty, and Savannah took the last watches. Although it meant getting a little wet, I suggested we use the bridge on the *Revenge*, as it was much higher than the other two boats, providing better visibility. Anchored in the cove as we were, the wind was pretty much blowing over the tops of the thick mangrove canopy.

I checked the anchor lights and generator before I turned in. Even though the wind and rain were heavy, I was asleep in minutes. I've slept in much worse places, under much worse conditions.

CHAPTER NINE

The alarm on my watch woke me two hours and twenty minutes later. I went barefoot into the galley, grabbed an apple and a mango, poured a thermos of coffee and donned my rain slicker, before heading up to the bridge. Jimmy was sitting on the port side bench seat and had the stereo turned on, but the volume down low. The singer was lamenting about a rising storm, which seemed appropriate.

"Who's that?" I asked. "Sounds pretty good."

"A local guy," Jimmy replied. "Plays at *Dockside* sometimes and over at *Porky's*. Name's Dan Sullivan."

"Never heard of him." I sat and listened to the song for a minute. He sang about battening the hatches, which caused me to grin. "Sullivan, huh? He Irish?"

"Probably his ancestors. He was born in Alaska, believe it or not. Been down here a few years now. The song's called *Storm Front*, one of his originals I recorded at the bar."

"I'll have to drop by and hear him play some time. Go ahead and get some rest. Tomorrow's gonna be a long, boring day."

As he got up he said, "You'd like Dan, he's into martial arts."

I spent the next two hours listening to the rain pouring on the overhead. It would let up at times and the stars would appear, but each band seemed to get more intense as the night wore on. When the easterly wind would let up, I could still hear music and occasional voices from the trawler in the next cove.

Just before zero-two-hundred, Rusty climbed up with a thermos of coffee. I'd just poured my last cup, so we sat together as the stars came back out again. We were talking about old times, when we were stationed together in Okinawa, when we both heard a splash.

I looked in the direction of the sound. "Came from over by that trawler."

A moment later, we heard the unmistakable sound of a small outboard start up. Rusty looked at me. "What kind of idiot goes out in a dinghy in this mess at zero-dark-thirty?"

"It's headed this way," I said as I stood up and got a powerful spotlight from under the bench seat. "You armed?"

As he pulled his Sig from under the back of his shirt, he responded, "Monkey got a climbing gear? You?"

I already had my own P-226 in my hand and nodded. "Step over onto Savannah's boat and get prone in the pulpit."

He was down the ladder and up to the bow of Savannah's boat much quicker than his size would dictate. I went to the pulpit of the *Revenge* and waited. We didn't have to wait long. About a hundred yards out, the outboard quit and was replaced by the sound of oars slapping the water. I let them get to within fifty feet of the bow, then hit them with the powerful spotlight.

"That's far enough!" I shouted. "What do you want?"

Baldy was in the bow of the inflatable dinghy and Crooked Nose was rowing. Both men froze in the blinding light. "Hey, cut the light, asshole."

"I'm only going to ask once more. What do you want?" I asked as Crooked Nose slowly dipped the oars once more, inching another five feet closer.

"Just wanted to see if y'all wanted to party, mister," Crooked Nose said as he slowly dipped the oars again and Baldy reached slowly into a bag at his feet.

They were inside my comfort zone and I wanted them to know it. As Baldy leaned forward for whatever was in the bag, I fired one shot through their starboard pontoon. Rusty fired a single round through the bottom, in front of Baldy's bag, causing him to jump backwards between the small bench seats.

"The next one goes between your eyes if you move even a fraction of an inch toward that bag!" Rusty shouted. "Your dink's gonna sink in about two minutes. I suggest you use that time to get your ugly asses back to that garbage scow and stay there."

Crooked Nose yanked on the pull cord and the little engine sprang to life. He quickly shifted to reverse and gunned it too hard, sending a wave over the transom of the small inflatable. He finally managed to get it turned around and raced back the way they'd come as fast as the sinking dinghy would go.

Jimmy, Josh, and Savannah were on the rear decks all asking what had happened as Rusty and I got back to the cockpit on the *Revenge*. I left Rusty to explain and went into the salon. When I came back out I was carrying my fins, mask, snorkel, a small but powerful underwater pen light, and a Drager LAR V rebreather. It's similar to scuba equipment, but without the noisy bubbles.

"It's a long swim, Jesse," Rusty said as he opened the transom door and then helped me strap on the rebreather.

"Gotta find out what they're up to," I said. "You got a better idea?" Everyone started talking at once, while I sat down on the bench seat by the transom door and put on my fins. "I'll go on the surface most of the way and drop below the surface about a hundred feet from their boat. If they're below deck, I should be able to pick up on what they're talking about."

"Hang on," Rusty said and disappeared into the salon. I did positive and negative pressure tests on the system and began the process of pre-breathing the unit to warm up the scrubber.

A moment later, he returned with a twenty foot coil of heavy anchor line. "This'll slow 'em down if we decide to move and they wanna follow."

I grinned at his ingenuity. Most trawlers are single engine and a length of rope can fowl a prop real quick, making them nearly dead in the water.

"Are you insane?" Savannah asked. "You can't see the end of your arm and the wind is kicking up white-caps out there."

"He'll be fine," Rusty said, slapping me on the back. As I stepped off the swim platform into the dark water I heard him add, "He went to night school."

On the surface, I took my bearings and submerged to go under the boat raft. Once clear I surfaced and could just make out the bobbing anchor float a hundred feet ahead. I swam straight for it, kicking hard in the darkness. Savannah was partly right, there were wind whipped waves outside the creek mouth, but we were between rain bands and as my eyes adjusted to what little light the stars provided, I was able to see pretty well.

I could see the trawler, well lit, about a quarter mile away in the next cove. I had two advantages, stealth with the rebreather, and the fact that with all the lights they had on board, they wouldn't be able to see anything in the water.

Using the small light underwater, I illuminated the dial on a wrist mounted compass for a few seconds. The needle and bezel would glow for a good thirty minutes after that. More than enough time to cover a quarter mile. The secret to swimming underwater at night is knowing how many kicks it takes to cover a known distance. We'd done it so many times in the Corps, it was habit.

Extending my right arm straight ahead, I put my left hand on my right elbow. This put the compass right in front of my face and my right arm ahead in case of floating debris. I started kicking, swimming against the wind and waves, so I allowed a foot less per right kick.

Ten minutes later stopped pretty close to where I'd wanted to. Replacing my snorkel with the second stage of the rebreather, I submerged, staying just three feet below the surface and followed the compass toward the trawler. Knowing I was close, I dove deeper to get below their hull and continued a few more feet.

I could sense the boat above me and chanced the mini-light for a second to get oriented. I'd overshot it a few feet and was under the port side, near the stern. I moved forward to amidships and came up under the hull. The sound of the generator in the engine room toward the stern drowned out just about anything I might hear through the hull. This part of most trawlers would be the crew quarters and I didn't think they'd be there. Just as I was about to move forward I heard a faint sound and a scrape on the hull. I held my breath and put my ear closer to the hull and heard it again. A muted moan and a sob. I listened for another minute but didn't hear anything more. I moved forward to where I guessed the galley would be. I began to hear voices through the hull. Fortunately it was an old wood hull. Sound travels through dense wood pretty well. Moving a few feet further toward the bow, the voices grew louder. I stopped and held my breath again, pushing my ear close to the hull.

I heard a voice distinctly through the hull. "I'm tellin' ya, Earl. It was the same guy that was at the bar the other night. And I'm pretty sure the boat on the left belonged to that blonde you was playing with."

A second deeper voice responded. "Get the Avon patched and reflated. It's about three miles around this island. We'll come up from behind 'em. And put the damn oars in the dinghy."

"Come on Earl," a third man said. "We got three women already and them guys got guns, too. Why don't we wait out the storm and get the hell outa here?"

The man named Earl bellowed, "Cause I said so, dammit! That blonde'll be worth more than all them other three combined. I ain't passing up a perfect chance to add ten grand to our haul. That third boat might have women aboard, too. Looked like a family type boat. Sides, I doubt they got guns like we got."

Sex slavers? I wondered in the inky darkness that surrounded me like a cocoon. *Three women?* Maybe that was what I heard in the crew quarters. I made my way to the propeller and uncoiled the anchor line. I tied it loosely around the propeller shaft, between the through hull seal and the propeller mount and released the rest to drop to the bottom. As soon as they put the boat in gear and started moving the line would get sucked up into the prop and with any luck either bend the shaft or break the mount.

It'd take them a while to patch their dinghy and reflate it. I had to get back to the others. I checked my dive watch and saw that it was still a good three hours until sunrise. I dove deep and took a reciprocal heading away from the trawler until I was a good hundred feet away. When I surfaced I switched back to my snorkel and looked back once more, before striking out for home.

Fifteen minutes later, I surfaced at the stern of the *Revenge*, three startled faces looking down at me and Rusty extending his hand. "Learn anything?"

I climbed onto the swim platform. "Yeah, we're in deep shit." Savannah wrapped a towel around my shoulders as I removed the rebreather and fins. "Remember that family that disappeared a couple weeks ago? Husband was found adrift, but the boat, his wife, and two daughters were never found?"

"Yeah," Rusty replied. "What about them?"

"I'm pretty sure the mother and daughters are aboard that trawler. And those guys are coming back with heavy firepower for more. Unlash the dinghy."

Drying off with the towel, I went into the salon and down to my stateroom. I quickly changed into dry clothes, knelt down by the foot of the bunk and punched in the code to unlock it. I raised the bunk, opened the chest and removed all four boxes, along with a fly rod case, then closed it back.

Carrying everything into the salon, where everyone had gathered, I placed the cases on the island counter. Josh had sent his daughters back to their boat. I picked up my Sig from the settee where I'd left it and handed it to Jimmy, then opened three of the boxes and handed Savannah, Tonia, and Josh identical Sigs, extra magazines and ammo.

"Those guys are planning to circle the island and come up on us from the stern. Rusty and I are gonna run an intercept. We'll go up the creek and find a place where we can try to stop them. If they get past us, don't hesitate to use these."

Tonia put the gun on the table like it burned her hands. "This is crazy!"

I turned to her husband. "Josh, these guys are in the sex slave trade. We don't have a lot of time. If they get to us, they'll kill the men and take the women, including your daughters, and sell them. Most likely to Arabs."

He looked stunned. Then he quietly picked up the gun Tonia had placed on the table and turned to his wife. "In case Captain McDermitt is right," he said gently. She looked at her husband, then to each of us, and finally out the porthole at their boat, where her daughters were.

She took the gun from her husband. "I don't even know how to use one of these."

"I do," Jimmy and Savannah chorused. Savannah inserted a magazine and quickly chambered a round.

Jimmy turned to me. "Go Skipper. We'll take care of things here."

Rusty came through the hatch with a long, nylon rope coiled around his shoulders. "Ready when you are, brother."

Carrying the fly rod case and the fourth box, Rusty and I went out to the cockpit with the others following us. My Zodiac was tied off to the stern, its twenty horse Yamaha idling quietly.

Rusty grinned when he saw the long case. "You plan to do some fly fishin'? Or did your new toy arrive?"

I grinned back at him. "You drive."

"Be careful, Skipper," Jimmy said.

"Get an email off to the Coast Guard, Jimmy. Give them the GPS coordinates of the trawler in the next cove and if you can find the names of the mother and daughters on the internet, tell them we have good reason to believe they're aboard."

"What are you going to do, Jesse?" Savannah asked with genuine concern.

"We'll try not to hurt them, but I'm not gonna let them get past us. It's the same four guys from *Dockside* the other night. When we come back, I'll flash a light three times. Please don't shoot us."

Rusty settled his portly frame in the stern and I took the forward seat, facing aft and untied the painter. Tossing it onto the swim platform, I pushed the bow away and Rusty put the engine in gear and moved slowly away from the *Revenge*.

"You wanna cut that light on?" Rusty said. "I can't see shit."

Opening the box, I removed two Pulsar Edge night vision optic headsets and handed him one, after first switching it on. "Here, see if this helps. Just don't look toward any bright lights."

He fitted the head strap on his bald head, settling the optics over his eyes. "Damn, man! Where'd you get these?"

"Had 'em shipped, along with the rifle." I put on, adjusted the straps and activated it. "Let's head up the creek about half a mile. We'll find a narrow spot and tie that line from side to side on the surface."

Rusty brought the quick Zodiac up on plane and headed upriver. "You noticed that too? When that guy backed up sudden, I seen his transom was loose."

"Yeah, with luck they'll be going fast enough to yank the engine right off the transom."

I opened the fly rod case and removed the new M-40A3 rifle. Reaching into the other box I removed the last item, a U.S. Optics MST-100 scope, and mounted it to the rifle's Picatinny rail. I'd used the M-40A1 with this same scope in the Corps. The Unertl designed scope also fit on the newer A3 rifle and I'd put about a hundred rounds through it on my island over the last couple of weeks.

Rusty slowed the Zodiac and pointed. "This looks good."

The creek narrowed just after the first bend and there were large mangroves on either side that we could use for cover. "Perfect. Put me off on the starboard side. I'll pay out the rope as you cross over."

He brought the Zodiac up on a sandbar created by a smaller creek and I climbed out. "Let's play it by ear. I don't want to kill them if we don't have to. Once they're stopped, you call out to them and I'll keep them covered. Be careful, they'll probably have a light on and it'll cause the optics to go white. You can get the Zodiac behind that dead fall over there and keep down behind it."

He slowly started across the creek and I uncoiled the rope until he reached the far side by a giant log. He pulled the Zodiac behind the large fallen mangrove and tied it off, then sloshed upriver and tied the rope around another one that was still standing.

"Tied off," he called out.

I pulled the slack out of the rope, leaving just enough so that it lay in the water, almost invisible. I tied my end off to a huge mangrove and then moved back to the sandbar, where a smaller tree trunk had fallen.

It had started raining again, as the next band came ashore. Neither Rusty, nor I were strangers to waiting in the rain. In Okinawa, back in the early eighties we had a Platoon Sergeant by the name of Russ Livingston that always said, "If it ain't rainin', it ain't trainin'." He trained us well.

A few minutes later, we could hear them, maybe half a mile away. Sound travels well across water, even out here in the Glades. A moment later, we could hear their voices. We were between two bends in the creek, about a quarter mile apart. I was counting on them rounding the bend and seeing a long straight stretch, turn off their light. I wanted it dark, when they hit the rope. That would give us the best advantage. That and surprise.

Through the night vision headset, I could see a glow lighting up the horizon around the next bend east of us. I raised the optics and waited. They came around the bend and just as I'd hoped, turned off their light, seeing that they had a long straight shot in a fairly wide creek. I lowered my headset and looked over at Rusty. He was just lowering his and looked over at me and nodded.

Through the grainy, green lens of the night vision goggles, I could see that there were three men on the boat, they must have left one on the trawler. They were coming toward us pretty fast, at least as fast as their old outboard could push them.

When they hit the rope stretched across the creek, it did a lot more than stop them. All three were big men and they were traveling at nearly twenty-five knots. The rope snagged the engine below the water line and jerked both it, and the rotten wood transom, com-pletely off, sending the dinghy into a sideways skid as the two men in front were launched over the bow. The guy on the tiller landed in the front, but managed to stay aboard.

One of the men yelled into the darkness. "What the hell'd you hit, Earl?" The dinghy had drifted thirty feet and the two men were swimming for it.

Just as the first man reached it, Rusty called out, "You in the water! Y'all don't follow directions very good. I distinctly remember telling you not to come back."

Earl was Baldy. He reached down into the bottom of the boat and picked up a flashlight. Looking through the scope with night vision goggles isn't easy and their boat was a hundred yards away.

In the Corps, we'd trained shooting under all kinds of conditions, including using night vision. I set the cross hairs on the man's hand as it came up. He had no idea where Rusty was and pointed the light straight toward shore, away from me. Before he could turn it on, I fired. The boom of the big rifle sounded like lightning, as the flashlight splintered in Earl's hand.

"You two in the water!" I shouted. "Your oars are floating ten feet behind you. One of you get them and the other get on the boat. You have ten seconds to decide."

Earl spun around in the dinghy and nearly fell out. He crawled to the stern and felt around. "Fuckin' engine's gone!"

"That's why I said get the oars. Five seconds." One of the men in the water started splashing around, feeling for the oars. "Five feet further upstream is one. The other one is to your left."

He found the first one and started toward the other one as Earl shouted, "You're gonna regret this, mister."

I put the scope on him and said, "If you don't do exactly what I say, I have no problem putting a hole in your forehead and leaving you for the gators. Now get that man out of the water."

He helped his friend into the boat, gasping. As he rolled over, I saw his face. It was Handsome. That left Crooked Nose in the water looking for the other oar.

"Straight ahead! Five feet!" Rusty shouted.

Crooked Nose found the second oar and was struggling to get to the dinghy with them. When he finally got to it, Earl took the oars and pulled him from the water.

The three men whispered amongst themselves, but I couldn't hear what they were saying. Finally Earl said, "You expect us to row back the way we came?"

"You're damn sure not going downriver toward our boats," I said. "Now real slowly, I want you to dump everything on that boat into the water."

I could see the indecision on Earl's face. He was wearing what looked like a gold doubloon necklace. "I can put a round dead center in that doubloon you're wearing, Earl. And there's nothing you can do to stop me."

He reached a hand to the necklace and realized that Rusty and I could see them somehow. Looking in my general direction he growled, "One of these days mister, you're gonna regret you ever met me."

"I already do. Now start dumping everything. Start with that revolver tucked in your pants. Real slow, Earl."

He reached with his left hand and pulled the pistol out with just his thumb and forefinger then tossed it into the water. As I watched, he removed a large duffle bag and dropped it over. Then several sets of handcuffs and finally two Uzi automatic machine pistols and dropped them overboard.

"Very good. I'm going to throw a line to you and you're going to tie it off to the bow of that dinghy. Do you understand?"

"Yeah," he grunted.

I untied the line from the mangrove tree, coiled it up, and threw it toward the dinghy, hitting Earl in the face. He almost fell out of the boat, but finally got his balance and handed it forward to Handsome.

"What are you gonna do?" Crooked Nose asked.

"I'm afraid you boys would get lost out here without help, so I'm gonna tow you back to your boat. Once you get there, I'm sinking your dinghy and as soon as this storm passes, you're going to weigh anchor and get out of here. Do you understand?"

"Yeah," Earl grunted again.

"Bravo!" I shouted over to Rusty. "Bring the Zodiac over and pick me up."

Rusty picked up that I didn't want them knowing our names. "Roger that, Alpha."

I watched the men as Rusty untied the other end of the rope, started the outboard and came across the creek. I climbed aboard and sat up high on the bow so I could see them clearly through the scope.

Rusty started the Zodiac moving forward. When the slack was out of the rope, he gave it more gas and we moved up the creek at about five knots. "Head up-river." I whispered. "Way upriver."

Ten minutes later, we got to the opening into the bay and instead of turning right to go to their boat, Rusty turned left and continued up Shark River. It took the three men another fifteen minutes before they real-ized they were going away from their boat, not toward it. By then we were three miles up the river at a fork where another creek joined in.

"Where the hell are you taking us?" Earl shouted.

I ignored him and told Rusty to take the right fork. Another mile we rounded a curve and came to a small island in the middle of the creek.

"Beach 'em on that island," I told Rusty.

He swung around the island dragging the hundred-foot rope across the beach on one side. When their dinghy bottomed out on the sand bar, Rusty shut off the engine.

"Get out!" I shouted.

The men hesitated, so I shot the dinghy on the port side pontoon. The loud report of the rifle was followed by the hissing of air escaping from the dinghy.

"I said get out!"

They scrambled onto the sand bar and I put another round in the starboard pontoon. The dinghy deflated quickly.

"Do any of you idiots know how this river got its name?" I asked.

When none of them answered, I continued, "It's called Shark River because it's infested with bull sharks. They're the only shark that can survive in fresh water. Any of you know anything about bull sharks?"

"They're big and they're man-eaters," Handsome said.

"That's right," I said. "We're going to leave you here on this little island now. You can use the dinghy as shelter from the storm. When it's over, I'll let the Coast Guard know where you are. Now, untie my line from your boat."

"One of these days mister," Earl grumbled as he untied the rope from the Zodiac and Rusty started the engine. "When you least expect it."

A moment later, we were up on plane headed downriver. We sped past the trawler and only slowed down when we got to the anchor buoy. I flashed my light at the boats three times and got a return flash from the bow of the *Revenge*.

Once aboard, Jimmy said that he got a return email from the Coast Guard saying that the Marine Patrol out of Flamingo was on the way in three boats and should arrive in less than an hour.

I pulled out a chart of the area and gave Jimmy the coordinates of the little island we put Earl and his buddies on and told him to email them back and let them know that only one man was aboard the trawler and the other three were stranded further up Shark River.

Dawn broke gray, rainy, and windy, an hour later. Clouds scudded across the sky constantly, but the rain still came in bands. Minutes later, we heard the sound of outboards racing up the river toward us. Jimmy and I went up onto the foredeck. Through the rain we could see blue lights flashing. Two of the boats held off, while the third came up to the bow.

One of the men on board looked up at us. "Are one of you Captain McDermitt?" He wore the bars of a Lieutenant on the collar of his yellow slicker.

"I am, Lieutenant. Did you get the update on where the three men are stranded?"

"Yes we did. How sure are you that the kidnap victims are aboard that trawler over there?"

"Not a hundred percent," I replied honestly. "At least not a hundred percent that it's the mother and daughters from that kidnapping last week."

"And how do you know this?"

"I swam over using a Drager rebreather and listened through the hull. I clearly heard them say they had three captives, but also wanted to kidnap the women we have aboard here."

"A rebreather? You some kind of Navy SEAL or something?"

"No, sir. Marine Force Recon."

"You said there was a man aboard the trawler? Is he armed?"

"The other three were," I replied. "I can't say for sure if that last one is or not. He's a meth head, by the way."

"Oh great," the Lieutenant said. "Just what I don't need, an armed tweaker. We'll be back to get your statements." Then he turned to the driver. "Let's go check it out, Sergeant." The three boats sped away toward the trawler. I hoped Tweaker didn't put up a fight.

Thirty minutes later, the rain stopped and we could see the trawler through the mist. We hadn't heard any gunshots, so that was good. One of the boats sped away, heading east.

Another fifteen minutes went by then we heard the unmistakable sound of a chopper coming in from the north. The orange and white markings on the MH-65 Dolphin were clear against the gray morning sky.

We watched as the chopper came to a hover just ahead of the trawler's bow about twenty feet above the water, the pilot doing a hell of a job holding her steady in the buffeting wind. A rescue swimmer jumped into the water and swam to the port side of the vessel, away from us, as the chopper moved to hover above the aft work deck and lowered a basket.

One by one, three people were lifted up in the basket from the work deck, the rescue swimmer hanging in a harness with the last person. The chopper swooped low over the water and passed directly in front of us. As they went by, the swimmer hung out the door and gave us a thumbs up, pumping his fist.

I heard the VHF radio squawk, "United States Coast Guard helo calling *M/V Gaspar's Revenge*."

I climbed quickly to the bridge and replied, "*Gaspar's Revenge* to Coast Guard chopper, go ahead."

"Congratulations, Captain. We have three souls aboard, hungry and slightly dehydrated, but they'll be alright. The Marine Patrol has four men in custody. Do you need assistance?"

A cheer went up from behind me in the cockpit. "Negative, Coast Guard. We're hunkered down for the storm. Thanks for letting us know they're alright."

He signed off just as the boat that had left the group earlier was returning. It didn't stop, but continued on toward the river across the bay. From my vantage point, I could see there were three men sitting on the deck with their arms behind their backs.

A moment later, a second boat left the trawler and took off after the first, with a fourth man sitting on the deck, trussed up like Earl and his buddies. After about fifteen minutes, the Lieutenant's boat came over and asked to tie up alongside. Once they were aboard, I invited everyone into the salon.

"For the record, Captain, those men stranded up on the island said you shot at them. Is that true?"

Rusty took a step toward him. "Lieutenant, are any of those men dead?"

"No. Why?"

"Jesse here was a sniper instructor in the Corps. If he'd shot at those men, they'd be dead. Did any of them see him shoot at them?"

The Lieutenant grinned. "No, they said they couldn't see anything. One said you shot his only flashlight right out of his hand in total darkness."

Rusty chuckled. "Well there ya go then. There's a storm blowing, maybe it was lightning."

The Sergeant laughed and the Lieutenant said, "Yeah, I suppose you're right. What made you think those women were aboard?"

I thought for a moment about how to answer that question then Savannah said, "Those same four men tried to kidnap me and my sister several days ago. Captain McDermitt and our Captain fought them off. Last night, when they entered the bay, Captain McDermitt recognized them and swam over to eavesdrop."

"That's a long swim in rough water," the Sergeant said. "But, for a Recon Marine, I guess it was like taking a Sunday stroll. Semper Fi."

I nodded to the Sergeant and the Lieutenant asked, "Anything else you'd care to add, Captain?"

"No, that's pretty much how it went down."

"Well, congratulations, sir. Mister Hendrickson, he's the husband and father, is being flown up to Tampa from Key West to rejoin his family. You're a hero."

"I'm no hero, Lieutenant. We only did what anyone else would do. Oh there is one other thing."

"What's that?"

"I guess you plan to move that trawler?"

"It will be impounded after the storm. Why?"

"You might want to put a diver in the water before moving her. He might find the prop is fowled."

The Lieutenant grinned and looked at his Sergeant. "You Marines don't take any chances, do you?"

"Not if we can help it," the Sergeant replied.

The Lieutenant said the Coast Guard would want to ask me some questions, once the storm blew over, so I gave him my address at Boot Key Harbor and they left. It'd been a long night, so I suggested everyone try to get some rest. Josh and Tonia volunteered to keep watch for a few hours and I went forward to get a shower and a nap.

CHAPTER TEN

I woke just before noon and went into the salon. Rusty and Savannah were watching the Weather Channel. Rusty looked up as I headed for the coffee maker. "Tropical Storm Irene made landfall on Isle of Youth this morning while all the excitement was going on. She's turned northwest and over mainland Cuba now."

"Just like Rusty predicted," Savannah added. I just nodded and poured coffee into my Force Recon mug.

"He ain't worth a plug nickel till he's had his lifer juice."

Savannah laughed. "I assume 'lifer juice' is a euphemism for coffee?"

"If that means does it mean coffee, yeah. Lifers drink it by the gallon."

"Did you two get any sleep?" I asked.

"I'll get all the sleep I need when they put me under the ground," my old friend replied.

"We stayed up with the Alexanders," Savannah added. "Rusty regaled us with your and his exploits in the Marines."

I sat down next to her on the settee. "You can pretty much bet that anything he told you is a sea story." I couldn't help but notice the warmth radiating from her bare thigh next to mine.

"Sea story? Another Marine euphemism?"

"Kinda like a tall tale," Rusty answered. "Gets better with each retelling. But actually, I kept to the truth. Well, pretty much."

Jimmy stumbled up the steps into the galley and went straight for the refrigerator. He got a bottle of orange juice, opened it and drank half in one long pull.

We talked about the pending storm and any other steps we could take to minimize damage. "If Jimmy's up to doing a little climbing," Rusty said, "some of the nearer mangroves have dead branches that we could cut away. Other than that, I'd say we're pretty well set."

We got to work and had all the dead branches trimmed away before nightfall, working between squalls. Once finished, we showered and gathered in the salon to get the latest update on the storm. It had just moved off the Cuban coastline and into the warm, shallow waters south of the Florida Straits and was upgraded to a category one hurricane, with sustained winds of seventy-six miles per hour.

By sunset, it had turned north by northeast and was heading straight for Key West. The east side of a hurricane is where the highest winds are usually located, which meant that the Middle Keys would take the brunt of the storm. We all hoped it wouldn't intensify over the Straits.

We assigned watch again and this time Josh insisted on being part of it, so we were able to cut it to only a two hour watch for each of us. We changed the order so that I had the zero-three-hundred watch and Rusty would take over after that. Knowing me as he did, he wasn't surprised when I came back up after he took over with another thermos of coffee.

Friday dawned gray and the rain was steady now as the hurricane got closer. The wind had intensified to a steady thirty knots. All our lines to the many mangrove trees were secure and with three boats lashed securely together we were actually very stable. Looking south out through the windshield, we could see fairly large waves and whitecaps building out on the bay. Sheltered in the narrow cove as we were, with trees to the east and west, there was only a little wave action and very little wind. But, you could hear it whistling through the treetops above us on either side.

Savannah came over from her boat, wearing her usual cutoff jeans, slicker, and bare feet. She brought her own thermos and offered us some of her Australian brew. We enjoyed it as we sat listening to the NOAA weather update on the VHF radio. It originated in Flamingo, which is out of range on normal radio frequencies, but only a little static on the VHF.

"It's headed straight to Key Weird," Rusty told Savannah. "Probably make landfall there in an hour or so. If it stays on that course and speed, the center's gonna hit here this afternoon."

"Are we prepared enough?"

Rusty looked around at the tree tops and ran his practiced eye over the many ropes holding us in place, then looked back at her. "Yeah, I'd say we're more than prepared. It won't be much of a blow and it'll probably be long gone by morning."

As the day grew longer, the wind grew stronger. The rain came off and on, but by afternoon, we'd grown used to being wet. At fifteen-hundred the NOAA update out of Flamingo said that the storm had made landfall on the mainland just north of Cape Sable. By then the wind was blowing steady out of the east at more than fifty knots and we'd long since cleared the bridge. The kids were trying not to be afraid, but the howl of the wind kept getting louder with every passing minute. The rain was coming down in sheets that made so much noise inside the salon, we had to shout to be heard above it.

Suddenly, all sound ceased outside just as Jimmy yelled, "I hope it doesn't get any worse!" His last two words were yelled into total silence and he started laughing.

"What happened?" the younger girl, Vanessa said, wide eyed with bewilderment.

"Eye of the storm," Rusty explained. "It's about a mile wide. If anyone wants to look outside, we have about four or five minutes before the wind starts from the opposite direction."

I couldn't resist and stepped out into the cockpit. The sun was shining and the sky was a deep blue directly above us. The others crowded through the hatch, everyone talking at once. I quickly climbed the ladder to the cockpit to check on everything. There was no damage. I looked quickly at our anchor lines and snub lines to the trees and everything looked good.

Looking south, I could see across the bay and just beyond it, a wall of clouds that seemed to go all the way up into space. "Here it comes! Everyone inside." I quickly climbed down the ladder and was the last one through the hatch. A moment later the howling wind was instantly upon us, torrents of rain beating on the starboard side portholes.

"I got an update while the eye was on us," Jimmy said. "It's increased forward speed to fifteen knots."

"That's good," Rusty shouted over the noise, as we all found places to sit. The two girls sat at the settee with Jimmy who kept them occupied with video games on the laptop. "It'll be off the coast way up to Fort Pierce just after midnight and by sunrise the sky here'll be clear as it was in the eye. That was something else, wasn't it?"

"You sound like you'd never seen it before," I said. "I thought you'd been through dozens of these storms."

"I have. That was just the first time I was in the eye."

The wind on the backside of the storm died away fast, as did the rain. By midnight, it was blowing about like it had been two days ago. I suggested everyone get some rest and since it was doubtful that anyone would be coming into the bay to escape the storm now that it was over, we didn't need a watch.

I was very tired and was asleep almost instantly. It seemed like only a few minutes later, when I sensed a change in the boat's attitude and was instantly awake again. A glance at my watch told me that I'd been sleeping over three hours.

As I started to get up, thinking one or more of the lines might have come loose, I heard the hatch open in the salon. I came out of bed instantly, pulling my Sig from under the pillow and pulled back the slide, checking to see if a round was still chambered, even though I knew there was.

Hearing footsteps quietly crossing the deck in the salon, I was about to yank open the hatch to my stateroom when I heard Savannah's voice. "Don't shoot me, Jesse."

I lowered the gun and opened the hatch. She was shrugging out of her rain slicker, barefoot as usual. But this time, she had nothing on under the slicker.

The smell of coffee roused me once more, as sunlight filtered through the overhead hatch. I moved my arm, Savannah was curled up with her head on my shoulder. I slowly eased my arm out from under her and rose from the bed, slipped my shorts on and padded barefoot to the galley.

"Jesse!" Rusty shouted from outside. I quickly moved to the hatch and went out to the cockpit. "Savannah's gone! The hatch to her cabin was open and she's gone. Is she on board the *Revenge*?"

"Will you calm down? You're gonna wake the dead. Yeah, she's inside."

His big shoulders rose as he sighed. "That's good, I didn't hear her get up this morning." He walked into the salon and started pouring a cup of coffee. "She in the head?" he whispered.

"Um, not exactly. I'll be right back."

I went down the steps to my stateroom. Savannah was awake, her hair in complete disarray. "I didn't think to bring any clothes," she said smiling coyly.

I opened one of the drawers in the dresser and pulled out an old pair of cutoffs and a belt. "Try these. We'll obviously have to cut a hole in the belt." I pulled out a *Dockside* tee-shirt I'd bought that was too small for me and tossed it on the bed with a grin. "Rusty's in the salon."

"Yeah, I heard him." She shimmied the shorts up over her hips, then pulled the tee-shirt on. We walked up into the galley. Jimmy and Josh were there with Rusty, all three of them staring and grinning.

"Thanks for the loan, Jesse," she said. "I think I'll go get a shower before breakfast."

The three men stepped aside to let her pass and once she closed the hatch, Rusty turned to me and grinned. "You old dog!"

"Shut up and pour me a coffee."

From that point on, we were inseparable, together day and night. For seven days.

CHAPTER ELEVEN

When I woke up on the eighth day after the storm, the memory of the recent hurricane was way in the back of my mind. I reached out for Savannah and she wasn't there. That side of the bed, already cold.

Probably getting us a cup of coffee, I thought. A few minutes later I got out of bed, went to the head and relieved my bladder. After washing and brushing my teeth, I went up to the salon. She wasn't there either.

Stepping out into the cockpit, I looked up at the bridge. We'd spent every morning since returning from Tarpon Bay sitting up there, enjoying our coffee and each other's company, watching the sun rise. Nothing.

I glanced up the dock toward *Dockside*, thinking she'd gone there to buy something and that's when I noticed her boat wasn't in its slip.

I leaped over the transom and ran down the dock. Her boat was gone. Her dinghy, which had been on the port side pier, was gone too. I ran to *Dockside*, yanked open the door and walked quickly across to Aaron's office. "Did Savannah leave?"

"Yeah, just after midnight. She said to give you this." He handed me a sealed envelope, which I tore open as I walked out of his office and out the back door into the early morning sunlight.

Dear Jesse,

I've really enjoyed spending time with you. I hope you'll forgive me sneaking out in the middle of the night. It's been a lot of fun, but it was time for me to move on.

Sharlee called while you were at the store yesterday. She's in Key Largo and ready to go home. To be honest it's time for me to do the same. Mom and Dad will be back next week, and I have responsibilities at home.

Please don't try to call or get in touch. I lied about having gone through a tough divorce. We're only separated. He wants to try again and to be honest, so do I. I'm sorry.

I'll remember you,
Savannah

I wadded it up and started to throw it in the water, but shoved it in my pocket instead. I walked back to the *Revenge* and started to untie her. Then I looked over at the Maverick tied up at the dinghy dock. I went aboard, gathered some clothes, canned food, loaded a cooler with beer and water, and carried them over to the Maverick. I started the engine, then went back and opened the bunk, pulled out the fly rod case and two of the water tight boxes and carried them to the Maverick also, after locking up the *Revenge*.

The Maverick already had bait casting rods, a cast net, spear gun, and snorkeling gear locked in a fish box, so I untied the lines, stepped aboard and backed her out. Minutes later, I was flying under the Seven Mile Bridge, heading to my island oasis.

I spent the next six nights camping on the island. By day, I snorkeled for lobster, speared fish, drank beer, and shot beer cans. I made a daily run to a nearby marina on Big Pine for more beer, water, and ice. On the second day, I noticed they had picks and shovels for sale, so I bought one of each.

I spent the next five mornings, standing in calf deep water, swinging the pick and shoveling sand, with the Maverick anchored where I'd dug the previous day. It was hard, wet work, but I enjoyed it immensely.

After five days, I had a trench from Harbor Channel that was wide enough and deep enough to get my skiff all the way up to the island, where I'd carved a notch right into dry land, bringing her up under the overhanging mangroves.

The afternoon of the seventh day since Savannah left, I was clearing the last of the underbrush in the middle of the island. My body was sore, scratched all to hell and I'd probably lost ten pounds. But, I felt good.

It'd been a while since I'd last worked hard in the hot sun, sweat dripping from my hair and body.

I heard an outboard far to the southeast, headed toward me. I walked down to where the Maverick was tied up and waded out to the stern, pulling my Sig from one of the watertight boxes. A few minutes later, Julie came flying through the cut in Cutoe Banks and turned sharply heading straight toward my island in her dad's skiff. I put the Sig back in the box.

Noticing the spoils from where I'd dug the channel and seeing me standing at the end of it, she idled straight up and cut the engine just before she got to the end. She threw me a line and I made it fast to a tree branch.

Julie climbed out and splashed across the water toward me. Throwing her arms around my neck. "We've been worried about you, Uncle Jesse."

"What'd I tell you about that 'uncle' stuff?"

"Screw you!" she shouted stepping away and putting her hands on her hips. "So it makes you feel old. You're the closest thing I have to an uncle and I will damn well call you that, if I want to."

Tears began to fill her eyes as she said it. She reminded me a lot of her mom, just then. Rusty's wife was hell on wheels and one of the toughest women I'd ever met. It took a lot to keep Rusty in line, back in the day.

"I'm sorry," I said sheepishly.

"Well you damn well should be! Aaron told dad what happened last week. He was going to come up here himself, but I told him it'd be better if I did."

I sat down on the gunwale of the Maverick and opened the cooler for a beer, then thought better of it and grabbed two bottles of water and gave her one.

"You know Jimmy had to cancel two charters this week? Are you coming home soon? Everyone's worried about you."

"What's to worry?" I said, with a bit too much bravado. "I just needed to get away for a while and get my head on straight. I'll be back in a day or two and I'll pay Jimmy for those missed charters."

"Look, Uncle Jesse, it's not just that. You have friends here. People who care about you. So you got dumped. It happens all the time, especially down here. Women, and men too, they come and go. They have a quick fling with a local and head back up north to the reality of their lives. Grow a pair and get over it. Do the same to them. You know what they say, 'When in the Keys'."

I laughed. "Grow a pair?"

She smiled. "Yeah, grow some balls and get back in the game."

"You remind me a lot of your mom."

"Yeah, dad says that all the time."

"She was wise beyond her years, too. Get on home, now, before it gets dark. I'll be back tomorrow. I just have a little more work to do here."

"What exactly are you doing, anyway?"

"Well, right here where we're standing will one day be a dock below my house. It won't be much of a house, maybe twenty feet by fifty feet, built up on stilts.' I pointed through the mangroves. "If you look through there, I've cleared the interior of the island and plan to start a garden."

"A garden? In coral rock and sand, with seawater just a couple feet under it? What do you plan to grow?"

"It can be done." Truth was, I hadn't thought about that part of it. "Well, it might take some work. Now, you get going. Darkness comes early these days."

"Uncle Jesse, I know the back country up here better than almost any man. There's not a cut, or coral head, I can't find blind folded."

"Okay then. Want to stay for supper?"

"What's on the grill?"

"Lobster and stone crab claws. The pantry's a little short on vegetables, though."

"Sounds good," she said. "I'll call dad and tell him I'll be a little late." She pulled a cell phone out of her pocket and opened it. Closing it, she stuck it back in her pocket. "Give me a boost up to that branch in the gumbo limbo behind you."

I boosted her up and she climbed another twenty feet up into the branches, before pulling the phone out again and punching some buttons. I heard her tell Rusty she was going to stay and have supper with me and would be home in a couple of hours. She listened for a minute and told him not to worry, I was okay and would be back tomorrow. Then she climbed down again.

I finished clearing some brush while she got a fire started and split the lobster tails with my heavy dive knife. We ate quickly, then she left. I hadn't seen my own kids in quite a few years now. Rusty and Julie were the closest thing I had to family and I knew it was wrong to take off and worry them like that.

I stoked more wood on the fire, adding some wet driftwood on top. I found that with the wet wood, the fire would burn for hours and keep the mosquitoes away. Then I stretched out in a hammock I'd bought at the marina on Big Pine and was soon fast asleep.

CHAPTER TWELVE

Winter passed quickly. Jimmy and I worked hard making the charter operation better. We were able to raise our prices twice and were still turning people away. By spring, as we rolled into the slow season, we began to get fewer dive charters.

I increased Jimmy's working wage to two-hundred and fifty dollars a charter and his weekly wage to five hundred to be available. He was a hard worker and his expertise in the technology department meant a lot more income to the boat.

After a very long investigation, Earl and his buddies were charged on three counts of kidnapping, four counts of assault and battery, one count of attempted murder, and multiple counts of sexual assault, including sexual assault on a child. They were all sentenced to life in prison.

I was called to appear as a prosecution witness. So were Savannah and Charlotte. It was a little awkward, meeting her husband outside the federal courthouse in Miami, but I just pretended she didn't mean anything.

As the summer doldrums rolled in and I celebrated my first year as a civilian, our charters became fewer still and mostly fishing. I preferred the dive charters, but to keep Jimmy flush with cash, we took out at least one or two fishing charters a week throughout the summer months.

Life at the marina slowed down in summer. Liveaboards pulled anchor and headed back up north to home ports. There were still quite a few tourists, mostly Floridians from the mainland, but they usually brought their own boats.

I spent the days doing routine maintenance on the *Revenge* with Jimmy. It didn't need much, but it kept us busy until early afternoon, when he'd head home and I'd take a few beers up to the bridge.

Occasionally someone would stop by and join me, usually Rusty, or one of the shrimpers. Sometimes, there'd be three or four of us sitting up there. It got to be a regular event.

Tourists who somehow found *Dockside* would wander out to the docks and occasionally strike up a conversation. Boot Key Harbor isn't visible from US-1, so the only tourists that found their way here, learned of its existence from someone else. I met a few women who came down to get away from whatever reality they were trapped in. A few managed to spend the night aboard the *Revenge*.

As summer drifted on, I started spending more of my days up on the island. To stay in shape, I did timed swims around another small island about three quarters of a mile to the northeast. Depending on the current, I'd either have a hard swim out or a hard swim back. When I wasn't on the island, I ran. *Dockside* is on Sombrero Boulevard, which is a one and a half mile loop around a park. Every morning, when I was in Marathon, I'd run the loop twice. Between the swimming and running, I managed to keep the beer from putting any extra weight on.

We didn't have any hurricane scares to speak of all summer long. By fall, we were back into lobster season and were doing three or four charters a week, half of which were photographers. In late September, I had Jimmy add a Thursday night dive to the website for photographers, and within a few days it was booked through the end of the year. Julie volunteered to help out on the night dives.

At first I thought that was going to be a problem, Jimmy and Julie working side by side. But, he'd given up on her and found a girlfriend, by the name of Angie. He introduced me to her one day. She was from Mobile, Alabama. Her dad was a shrimper and they'd just moved back to Key West from there and bought his own shrimp trawler.

On the evening of November 10th, instead of sitting up on the bridge and it being a Friday, I put on shoes and headed over to the *Anchor*. It wasn't just any Friday. November 10th is the birthday of the Marine

Corps. Rusty said he was planning a celebration and I'd better be there.

Since it was only a half mile, going through the woods, but mostly because the International wasn't running again, I walked over. I probably should replace the old truck, but then I'd be constantly worried about getting a ding in the door, or someone stealing it.

Coming out of the woods, across the canal from the *Anchor*, I could see that the parking lot was already more than half full and there were a dozen or so skiffs at the rickety dock. I walked around the end of the canal, across the yard, and into the bar.

"Hey, Jesse!" Rusty shouted from behind the bar. "Glad you made it. Now I won't be the oldest."

He slid a cold Red Stripe in front of me as I sat down in my usual spot at the far end of the bar. By the wall. Facing the door. It's true what they say, old habits die hard. "I'm only two weeks older than you, brother." I lifted my beer bottle and grinned. "Semper Fi."

"There'll be a few other Jarheads in tonight," Rusty said. "And a special guest is in town from the mainland."

"Who?"

"Sergeant Livingston just blew in this afternoon." He still called Russ Sergeant, even though he'd been promoted to Staff Sergeant, then left the Corps to hunt for treasure. He and I became close friends after Rusty left the Corps and came down here from time to time over the years. We both loved diving and on one dive many years back, we found a whole clump of silver coins. That's when the bug bit him.

"Russ is in town? How long's he staying?"

A familiar voice boomed from the open doorway. "Jesse, you old camel humper!"

I got up from my stool and met him half way across the bar. "Who the hell are you calling old, Russ? You looked in the mirror lately? How long's it been?"

"Too long, my brother from another mother. Damn, I been here thirty seconds already and nobody's bought me a beer yet."

We sat down at the bar and Rusty put another cold beer in front of Russ and leaned on the bar. "Now, what the hell were you telling me on the phone about your kid being in the Navy?"

"True as I sit here, Rusty. Graduated Annapolis in '97 and could have been a Second Lieutenant. Said the Corps wasn't big enough for both of us and became an Ensign instead. I gave him his first salute, anyway. He's a SEAL now."

"A SEAL?" I asked.

"Yep, picked up Lieutenant Commander just last week, too."

"From Ensign to Lieutenant Commander in under four years?" How's that possible?" I asked.

"Graduated top of his class, commissioned an Ensign, and promoted to Lieutenant JG in less than a month. Picked up Lieutenant a year later. Musta got it from his momma."

I raised my beer bottle in toast. "To Commander Livingston."

We clinked the necks of our beers together. I hadn't seen Russ's son since he was little. It was good to hear that he was making his own way in life and doing so well.

"So, how long are you down here for?" I asked Russ.

"Just a few days. Got a lead on a wreck I've been researching."

"Spanish galleon?" Rusty asked.

"No, actually a Civil War wreck. Meeting a guy tomorrow that's supposed to be related to someone that was on board when she sank. Probably won't get anywhere, but I figured I could schmooze the guy a little and drop in and see you guys."

"Have enough time to go diving?" I asked.

"Rusty told me you had a dive boat," Russ replied. "Yeah, we can blow some bubbles. You in, Rusty?"

"Can't," Rusty replied as Jimmy and Angie walked toward us from the front door of the bar. "Julie's visiting a friend on Long Key this weekend."

"Just the two of us then?" he asked turning back to me. "Tomorrow?"

As Jimmy and Angie reached the bar, I said, "Russ, meet my first mate, Jimmy Saunders and his girlfriend, Angie Trent." They shook hands and I added, "Russ and I served together in the eighties. Do we have anything on the books for tomorrow, Jimmy?"

"No, man. Nothing till Tuesday."

"Great! Russ and I are gonna dive Conrad tomorrow."

"Take your bags, man, that reef's loaded with bugs. Nice to meet ya, Russ." The two went over to a table and joined another young couple.

"That the best you can do for a mate down here?" Russ asked. "I could smell the ganja when he walked in."

"Jimmy's alright," I said. "He knows boats and the water better than anyone else around here. Works hard, never complains, and doesn't bring it on the boat. Let's go out tomorrow afternoon. I have a compressor on board, so we can make an afternoon dive, eat supper aboard, then a night dive. You remember Conrad?"

He laughed. "Yeah, I sure do. That was one crazy fun day." Then he got melancholy and added, "Too bad the news we got that night ruined it."

Russ and I found that little patch reef many years ago, in late '83. We'd just returned from Lebanon as part of a multinational peace keeping force and came down to visit Rusty and to escape the visions and memories of what happened there.

We talked a while longer, as the bar filled up. Rusty introduced us to a few other Marines from all over the Keys. Having lived here all his life, he probably knew everyone up and down the island chain. One was a retired Sergeant Major, by the name of Kevin Landeros, who owned a diving school up in Key Largo. He looked to be in his early sixties, which I confirmed when I noticed a Vietnam Vet tattoo on his forearm.

Always looking for more contacts in the business, I bought him a beer and invited him to a table. He and I took one in the corner and exchanged the usual questions. When did you retire? Where were you stationed? Did you ever know so and so? As it turned out, we knew someone in common. A range coach I served with in '98, just before I retired.

"I served with Tank in the latter part of Vietnam," Kevin said. "Any idea where he might have retired to? Be good to see him again."

"Still active duty as far as I know," I replied. "I was a Scout/Sniper Instructor with Second Force Recon in ninety-seven and ninety-eight. He was a Range Coach then. I think the Corps just ran out of billets to put Tank in. He was at my retirement."

"Active duty? He's got to be close to thirty years," he said, meaning that Tank was near thirty years in the Corps.

"Normally, the Corps would retire a man at thirty," I said. "Unless he had a shot at becoming Sergeant Major of the Marine Corps. But, with that little blue ribbon on the top of his rack, there's no way they'd do it. Good PR to have an active duty Medal of Honor recipient. I think he's the only one."

"Only one I know of," Kevin said. "Rusty said you have a charter boat down here."

"Yeah, just bought it last year and doing pretty good. My First Mate is something of a computer and photography guru. We specialize in photography charters."

"Good idea carving out a niche. Separates you from every other Bubba that comes down here and tries to start a business. What kinda boat?"

"It's a Rampage forty-five. We do some fishing charters, too. But, I prefer the divers."

"That's quite a boat. Get my address from Rusty and ship me a box of flyers. One of my instructors teaches an advanced underwater photography course. Might be able to send some customers your way."

"Thanks, I'll do that and you do the same. The photographers seem to be the better clients. Always mindful not to damage my equipment."

"That's because they have pretty expensive stuff, too. Some of the equipment my Instructor has will set you back more than a new Cadillac."

Russ joined us and we discussed the dive we had planned and how many lobster we might get. Then Rusty rang the old ship's bell behind the bar and the back door opened. Two men wheeled a cart in with a large cake and an NCO sword on it. The cake was adorned with the Marine emblem.

Kevin being the oldest Marine in attendance joined a young man I hadn't met yet, who couldn't have been more than twenty-five. It turned out, he was an active duty Marine, home on leave. The two of them performed the cake cutting ritual that marks birthday celebrations all over the world on this particular day. After each man used the NCO sword to cut a slice, he presented it to the other. Then one of the guys that wheeled it in took over and served the rest, including all those in attendance that weren't Marines.

It was a lot of fun and the evening passed quickly. I told Kevin I'd get some flyers up to him, or maybe deliver them myself, as I wanted to check out his school.

Just before midnight, I slipped out quietly and made my way back to *Dockside* and my boat. I grabbed a couple of beers from the refrigerator in the galley and went up to the bridge to catch the end of *Dockside Folly*.

CHAPTER THIRTEEN

The following morning, I was up early and took a thermos of coffee up to the bridge to watch the sunrise. The early morning sounds of the marina are a great way to start the day. There wasn't a cloud in the sky as the sun began to rise over the mangroves that lined the east side of the harbor. Gulls wheeled and dove on baitfish and a slight breeze caused sailboats to move and their rigging to clank against the aluminum masts. Even the occasional car horn on US-1 filtered through the trees seemed tranquil.

I reflected back on the nearly eighteen months since I left the structured military life and joined this group of island dwellers and misfits. While it was a relaxing lifestyle, I'd only felt completely in my element during the hurricane when bad people threatened. I'd have to work on that, learn to relax a little more. But, like I said, old habits die hard. I sometimes catch myself evaluating a simple parking lot for possible threats, choke points, and other hidden dangers that are simply not there.

"Figured you'd be up," a familiar voice called, interrupting my thoughts.

I looked down at the dock. "Come aboard, Russ." I climbed down the ladder to the cockpit.

"Wanted to see your boat. Got any more of that lifer juice?"

"Come inside," I replied, opening the hatch to the salon.

He let out a low whistle when he stepped up into the salon and looked around. "This is a long way from the squad bay on Oki."

I poured him a mug of coffee in the galley as he looked around. "What's she got for power?"

I grinned. "I bought her at a Coast Guard auction. She was seized from drug runners. Just below us are a pair of one-thousand and fifteen horsepower Cats, that'll push her to about forty-five knots."

After giving him the nickel tour, we went up to the bridge and relaxed, while talking about old times and treasure hunting. Since neither of us had eaten breakfast we walked over to *Dockside* for the early buffet.

"We going out in the Rampage?" he asked after breakfast.

"Yeah, but if you don't have anything to do this morning, I thought you might like to run out to the back country in the skiff. I own an island up in the Contents."

"You own an island? Why?"

"You'll like it. I plan to build a house on it one day. Great fishing and a natural deep-water channel just a few yards away that's loaded with stone crab."

He stood up. "Lead on, brother."

After grabbing his snorkeling equipment from his pickup, we took the Maverick and headed north. Twenty minutes later, we anchored in Harbor Channel and free dove for stone crab the rest of the morning. Russ found a large cluster of chitons, a segmented mollusk that attaches to rock and eats algae. He pried about a dozen of the two-inch long animals from the rock and put them in his bag. We each caught a lobster and I speared two yellowtail snapper.

Once we got back aboard the skiff, I asked about the chitons. I knew people in the Philippines considered them a delicacy, but had never tried one.

"They taste a little like oyster," Russ explained. "Great in stews, or grilled on the shell."

"I have a small grill on the island. Let's have some lunch and I'll show you around."

I took the Maverick up the shallow channel I dug, pulled up under the mangroves, tied the skiff off, and went ashore. The grill was right where I'd left it. We put some dried driftwood in it and started a fire. While I cleaned the fish and lobster, Russ explored the island, which didn't take very long.

I had the fish and lobster on the grill when he got back. Russ placed the chitons around the lobster tails upside down. "Watch this." They slowly rolled themselves into balls when they were exposed to the heat.

After a few minutes they unrolled again, the body having cooked in its own juices.

Using banana leaves from one of the many trees on the island for plates, we sat on the trunk of a large lignum vitae tree that had fallen years ago. We were on the west side of the island, overlooking the sand bar eating with our fingers. There's nothing that compares to eating fresh seafood, straight from the sea.

"Where do you plan to build this house of yours?" Russ asked.

"Right above where the skiff is. On stilts."

He looked around the island as we finished our lunch. "Yeah, I can see it. I'd like to do something like this myself one of these days."

We got back to Marathon about an hour later, stuffed and feeling good. Whenever Russ and I would get together, we always enjoyed one another's company. When we first met in Okinawa, I was a lowly Lance Corporal and Russ was my Platoon Sergeant. In training, he was all business and rode us hard. But after hours, we'd talk about fishing and diving. Originally from Philadelphia, he'd visited south Florida in the late seventies and fell in love with it. When Rusty transferred in, Russ instantly befriended him, also. He pumped us for every bit of information about both the Keys and the southwest coast, where I was from.

In the summer of eighty-two, he went back to Camp Lejeune, but we kept in touch. I wound up there a few months later and we took leave together to go diving. We dove near my home the first few days then he suggested we try the east coast. Beach diving in Fort Pierce for lobster we found treasure, completely by accident.

I'd pulled a large rock out of the way to get at a lobster. While I was trying to catch it, Russ studied the rock. It turned out to be two-hundred and fifty-six silver bars, worth about a hundred grand.

Russ was hooked and even though he'd just been promoted to Staff Sergeant, he left the Marine Corps when his enlistment was up the next spring. He'd been chasing treasure ever since.

"Have you dived Conrad recently," Russ asked.

"A few times. Since I moved down here, I found out it wasn't some unknown new reef we'd just stumbled on. Not many people know about it, outside of the locals, though. It's the wreck site of a British ship the Adelaide Baker."

The mere mention of a ship wreck riveted his attention. I continued, "She went down in 1889, carrying lumber up to Savannah. Struck the edge of Coffin's Patch and spilled most of her granite ballast. Salvagers rescued the crew and later salvaged most of the lumber."

"No treasure, huh?"

"No, unless you count all those lobster."

At fifteen-hundred, I started the engines and we cast off. It didn't take long to reach the reef and the day couldn't be better, not a cloud in sight. At only twenty or twenty-five feet, we'd have an hour of bottom time and being a Saturday evening, we had the whole reef to ourselves. Once we were anchored on the south side of the reef, I ran up the red and white dive flag then we donned our scuba gear, and slipped into the water.

Reaching the reef, we split up and went around it in opposite directions. While most recreational divers would think this to be a bad idea, Russ and I were both former Recon divers and had made hundreds, maybe thousands of solo dives in dark and murky water. Here, the water was gin clear and the sun was shining.

Conrad is a really beautiful reef, with lots of tropical fish, coral, and sea fans. While looking for the telltale lobster antennae poking out of cracks and crevices, I enjoyed the reef's beauty.

Within minutes, though, I became wrapped up in the hunt, spotting several lobster wedged into a single hole. I used a tickle stick to coax each one out, one at a time. Two were obviously too small, but a third one was equally obvious to be of legal size. And then some. Into the bag he went and I continued around the edge of the reef, looking for more.

Before long, I realized I was going to catch my limit easily and released a few of the smaller legal sized ones. Within forty minutes, I met up with Russ on the far side of the reef, with four really big lobster in my bag. Russ was grinning around his second stage as he approached. He held up his hand with four fingers extended, then held both hands two feet apart, telling me he'd caught four big ones, also.

Back on the boat, we emptied our bags into a fish box in the deck that I'd already filled with sea water. There was no need to measure a single one, they were all monsters. We high fived each other, then hooked the tanks up to be refilled, as the sun started to slip toward the western horizon.

While the tanks filled, we climbed up to the bridge with a bowl of sliced fruit, sandwiches, and a half dozen bottles of water. We'd no sooner sat down when I saw a boat heading toward us. A moment later, I recognized it as a Marine Patrol boat.

"You have your fishing license and lobster stamp handy?" I asked. "We're gonna have company in a few minutes."

"Down below in my go bag."

We climbed down to the cockpit and as Russ went inside, I retrieved my wallet from a stash spot inside the engine room hatch. The Marine Patrol boat pulled up alongside and the officer on board looked my boat over, then reached to tie off to the stern port cleat. I put my hand on the cleat and said, "You need to ask first."

"Excuse me?" the officer said.

"It's common courtesy to ask, before tying off."

"It might be courtesy. But it's not the law."

"You're a state law enforcement officer, not federal. While the Coast Guard can board without permission, you need probable cause."

"This is a fishing boat, Captain. That's probable cause."

Russ came out of the cabin just then and said, "No officer, it's not. While it may resemble a fishing boat, do you see any fishing tackle, any rods, any fish guts, or blood? Any boat can be used for any purpose. The captain is only asking that you show a little professional courtesy."

The officer looked from Russ back to me and finally said, "May I come aboard."

"Yes, you may," I responded removing my hand from the cleat. "See, that wasn't so hard."

He tied off quickly and stepped over. "I need to see your identification and boat...."

I cut him off. "All right here." I handed him my driver's license, Captain's papers, registration, and fishing license, with lobster stamp. Russ handed his own over, also.

"Where are you out of?"

"Boot Key Harbor," I replied.

"I haven't seen you around before. How long have you been here? And if you're not a fishing boat, why are you handing me a fishing license?"

"I've been here a year and a half and run charters out of Boot Key Harbor, docked at *Dockside*. Today, we're a pleasure boat, just two buddies catching lobster." With that, Russ opened the fish box, showing him the eight huge lobster we caught.

"You said you weren't fishing." The officer said to Russ.

"No, I asked if you saw anything that would indicate we were engaged in fishing, which would give you probable cause to board without consent." Russ was enjoying this as much as I was.

The officer realized we knew the regulations as well as anyone and it was unlikely he'd find anything to cite us for. He glanced at the lobster in the fish box and handed our papers back. "Being a smart ass isn't always a good idea," he said. "But, since I'm in a good mood, I'll just leave you gentlemen be."

With that, he stepped back across to his own boat, untied it and started the engines. As he backed away, Russ and I both saluted him with our left hands and he returned the salute with his right, oblivious to the insult, which caused us to laugh as he roared away.

We climbed back up to the bridge and relaxed with another bottle of water, waiting for the tanks to fill, and watched the sun set slowly into the sea. As it neared the horizon and the sky darkened, the sun seemed to dim and flatten out on the bottom and the sky to the west turned to a pale orange.

I turned on the anchor light, cockpit lights, and the transom lights, before we reentered the water. We agreed before submerging that since we were only four short of our limit, we'd measure and keep all the legal ones we caught then release all but the four largest when we meet up on the other side.

Submerging at the stern, the bottom was illuminated by the powerful lights just below the waterline on the transom. We finned toward the reef, turning on our underwater flashlights then split up again when we got to the edge of the reef. As I finned slowly around the left side, I moved my light up and down the reef.

Most of the colorful tropicals were gone, nestled into little crooks and crannies for the night. The night creatures were out now. Soldierfish, squirrelfish, crabs, and shrimp of all kinds. I noticed a queen parrotfish, fully wrapped in its mucus cocoon. Within minutes, I caught the first bug and as I moved around the reef I caught seven more before meeting up with Russ on the other side. As we settled to the bottom, Russ held up three fingers on one hand above five fingers on his other.

We'd developed hand signals over the years and I knew instantly what he meant, he had three lobster over five inches carapace length. I replied with two fingers over five. That meant that everything in both bags under five inches could be released. We each started pulling bugs out of our bags measuring them and either releasing them, or putting them back in. We released six that although they were legal, were smaller than everything else we had.

I put my two in his bag, then we went through the process again, looking for the one that would be pardoned. After measuring each of them again, as we transferred them into my bag, we soon identified the smallest and let him join his buddies on the reef.

Back on the surface, we boarded the *Revenge* and added the four to the fish box. I turned on the fresh water wash down pump and rinsed our gear, then myself. While Russ was rinsing off, I climbed up to the bridge and started the engines.

"Russ," I yelled down, "there's a small cooler on the deck inside the hanging closet in the salon. Grab a few beers from the fridge before you come up."

He gave me a thumbs up and went into the salon as I put the engines in gear and eased forward, engaging the anchor windlass and drawing up the anchor line as I went.

"Here ya go, Jesse," Russ said as he handed up the cooler. "I'll get the anchor."

I turned on the forward spotlight and pointed it toward the pulpit. I had red tape around the anchor line, five feet before the chain and when it appeared, I disengaged the windlass, until he got up there. It only took him a second to lift the anchor and chain and put it in place then I engaged the windlass to take the slack out of the anchor line. When Russ was back up on the bridge, I pushed the throttles forward, bringing the big boat up onto plane and turning west.

"That was fun," Russ said. "Most of my dives these days are with metal detectors and shovels."

"Ever think you made the wrong move?"

He thought for a moment. "There are times, yeah. Like last night, hanging out with other Jarheads. I could be retired with a full thirty, this year. But I love what I do, it's fun and I'm my own boss. There's a lot to be said for that."

"It's been a year and a half for me. Still going through the change, I guess."

"Looking for dangerous situations where there aren't any?"

"Yeah, something like that."

"That means I did my job right. I had a Platoon Sergeant in seventy-one, right after I finished Infantry training and went to First ANGLICO. Guy by the name of Quick. 'Head on a swivel', he pounded into us. His training kept a lot of us alive in 'Nam."

I turned north around East Sister Rock and slowed down, dropping down off plane. "Now there's an island home for ya," Russ said, admiring the home on the little island at the mouth of Sister Creek.

"Yeah, he's close enough that he's got electricity and running water," I said, as we entered the creek. "Where I'm at, I'll have to rely on a rain cistern and battery power."

We wound our way up the creek into Boot Key Harbor. Russ climbed down to tie us off, as I swung the bow away from the docks. Standing and facing aft, I used the throttle controls to align the big boat and slowly back into the slip.

It sounded like a pretty lively crowd was at *Dockside*, even for a Saturday night. I climbed down and connected the shore power and water lines to the boat. Russ was looking toward the bar and listening to the music.

"The guest head should have everything you need, Russ. Why don't we get cleaned up and go have a beer?"

"It's like you're reading my mind, old son."

We cleaned the lobster and got cleaned up ourselves. Then we headed over to the bar to see what all the excitement was about. The place was nearly packed, but we managed to find a table in the corner that wasn't occupied. Funny how the best seats in most bars are usually empty. Robin was behind the bar and when I caught her eye, I held up two fingers and she nodded. A moment later a new waitress appeared with two ice cold Red Stripes.

"I'm Madison," she said placing the bottles on coasters. "Can I get you gentlemen anything else?"

She was pretty and half Russ's age, but that didn't stop him. "Can I get something that's not on the menu?"

To her credit, she smiled and countered him. "I'd have to check with Tom, the cook."

Russ laughed and handed her a ten, telling her to keep the change and keep the beer flowing.

"Hey, Madison," I said. "Why's it so crowded tonight?"

"It's Dan Sullivan's last night on stage. He's leaving in two weeks, to sail the Caribbean."

I looked up at the empty stage. He was apparently taking a break. This was the guy Jimmy had mentioned and I'd wanted to meet. "Do me a favor, Madison. Send him a pint of Guinness and tell him it's from a fellow Irishman."

She disappeared and Russ asked, "What was that all about?"

"Just a guy I wanted to meet. Some kinda local celebrity."

A moment later, a tall man with curly dark hair slightly tinged red, and a thick mustache stepped up to the table. "Dia dhaoibh."

My grandpa spoke the ancient Irish Gaelic fluently, but I hadn't heard it in many years. I struggled for a second to remember the correct response. I lifted my bottle and replied, "Dia is Muire dhuit."

"Ah, a real Irishman among us. Name's Dan. Dan Sullivan." I stood and took the hand he offered.

"Jesse McDermitt. And this is Russ Livingston." He shook Russ's hand and I invited him to have a seat.

"My first mate was playing some of your music on the boat some time ago. Jimmy Saunders."

"Jimmy's your mate? He did some recording for me a few months back. Smart guy."

We talked for a few more minutes before Dan had to get back up on stage. It turned out that Jimmy was right, I liked the guy. His music was simple, just his voice and guitar, and some of the stories he told in his songs were great. At the end of his set, he did the song I'd heard Jimmy playing about an approaching storm front. When he took his next break, he stopped by our table again and I asked him about it.

"It's called *Stormfront*, my newest song. Ya like it?"

"Yeah," I replied. "Jimmy was playing it while we were anchored in Tarpon Bay riding out Hurricane Irene. He also mentioned you were into martial arts."

"Been practicing Taekwondo, yeah. You?"

"I guess you could say mixed martial arts. I was a LINE instructor in the Marine Corps for a time."

"Line? What's that?"

"The Corps is big on acronyms," Russ said. "It means Linear Infighting Neural Override Engagement."

"Yeah, I can see where an acronym would work better there," Dan said with a grin. "You were both in the Marines?"

"Yeah," I replied. "Russ was once my boss."

"Well, a bonny Veterans Day to ya," he said, lifting his beer.

He asked more about what LINE was and I explained it was developed for Marines and some Special Forces Soldiers for close quarter combat, usually when fatigued and in low light situations, while wearing full combat gear, employing lethal strikes and holds.

"Why would you want to teach martial arts to people who are tired and it's dark outside?" he asked.

"Well, it's not really martial arts in the way most people know it. We don't teach how to defend, or incapacitate. It's mostly how to kill quickly and quietly."

"Think you could tone it down a bit and not kill a sparring partner?" he asked.

"Well, none of my trainees walked away dead."

He laughed. "I like you, Irishman. We'll have to get together and share some techniques in the ring."

"Sure. That'd be fun. But, I heard you're leaving soon."

"In two weeks, I'm sailing for the Leewards, to bring Conch music to the heathens."

"Drop by the boat tomorrow. Slip number ten."

"I'll do that," he said, as he stood up. "Right now, gotta get back to work."

As he went back up on stage I saw Aaron come out of the office and start to go behind the bar. When he saw me and Russ, he stopped and went back into his office. A moment later he came out, carrying a folded newspaper, heading straight for our table.

"Did you see the Keynoter, Jesse?"

"Hey Aaron," I replied. "Have a seat. This is an old friend, Russ Livingston. Russ, meet Aaron, the manager."

Aaron nodded at Russ and asked again, "Did you see the paper?"

"The Keynoter? Not unless I have a fish to wrap. What's up?"

By way of an answer he opened the paper to the front page. There was a picture, a mug shot actually, but it was obviously Earl. The headline read, 'Sex Slaver Escapes Prison'.

"He was being transferred from the federal prison in Miami, up to Raiford. The van was in a wreck and he escaped."

I read the story. The wreck happened on US-27, just north of Alligator Alley. There was a guard and a driver, plus two inmates in the van. Apparently, Earl took advantage of the situation and killed the guard and the other prisoner.

Witnesses at the scene said he fled on foot into the swamp. The driver was knocked unconscious and was in critical condition at Northwest Medical Center in Margate, near Fort Lauderdale. A Division of Prisons spokesman said that the dead officer's weapon was not recovered at the scene and Earl Hailey was to be considered armed and extremely dangerous. It happened yesterday.

I handed the paper back and Russ asked, "Who's this Earl Hailey?"

Before I could say anything, Aaron sat down and pointed to Earl's picture. "Jesse was instrumental in his being captured with three kidnapped women. Well, one woman and her two teenage daughters. Hailey and his friends were all convicted and got life sentences. Jesse left three of them stranded up Shark River during the hurricane." Turning to me, Aaron asked, "You think he'll come back down here?"

"I seriously doubt it." However, in the back of my mind, I thought it a pretty good possibility. I was number one on Earl's payback list.

"You left them stranded in the 'Glades during a hurricane?" Russ asked. "You must be getting soft."

I ignored Russ. "Thanks for letting me know, Aaron. I wouldn't worry about Earl. He's probably half way to Mexico."

Russ and I listened to Dan's songs a while longer, but he had to get up early to meet someone on Big Pine for breakfast. After he left, I wandered down the dock to the *Revenge*. Truth is, I was pretty certain Earl would be back here, if he wasn't here already.

I was glad Jimmy and Rusty had convinced me of the need for a security system. But even the best system can be thwarted. Standing next to my boat, I studied the water. If anyone was aboard, their slightest move would cause the tiniest ripple as the boat moved. After a moment, I was sure nobody was aboard and stepped down into the cockpit.

I opened the hatch, went inside and turned off the alarm. I crossed the salon and went down to my stateroom, punched in the key code to raise the bunk and retrieved one of the Sigs. I checked the chamber, inserted a loaded magazine, put it in a clip holster and tucked it into the waistband of my pants, under my shirt.

Grabbing a cooler, I put a couple of Dos Equis in it and went up to the bridge. After a few minutes, I began to relax. The more I thought about it, the less I thought Earl would return. There's only one way in and one way out of the Keys. He's bound to know this and know that the authorities would be looking for him here. It would be foolhardy to return here.

"Nice boat," came a voice intruding on my thoughts.

I looked down and saw a short haired woman a few years younger than me, late twenties or early thirties maybe. She was tall, slim and attractive. Her hair was a light brown with lighter highlights, longer in the front angling up to the back.

"Thanks," I said. "Just a working boat, though."

"Are you the crew? Or do you own it?"

"Both," I replied with my best smile. When in the Keys...

CHAPTER FOURTEEN

Her name was Barbara, an elementary school teacher from up the coast a couple of hundred miles. She'd driven down by herself for the weekend, just to watch the sunsets and found *Dockside* by accident while looking for a beach.

The smell of coffee and bacon woke me the next morning. When I looked at my watch, it was already zero-eight-hundred. I rarely sleep that late. Either I was getting old, or Barbara wore me out. Maybe both.

I got up, pulled on my boxers and walked up the steps to the galley. "Hope you don't mind," she said turning toward me. "I woke up very hungry." Her hair was tousled and she was wearing my tee-shirt, which barely covered her backside. I couldn't help notice it was bare, which caused a stirring in my groin.

I stepped up behind her, reached around and ran my hands over her taut, flat belly, pressing myself tightly against her. "I woke up hungry, too." She turned the alcohol stove off and moved the half cooked bacon off the burner then turned inside my embrace and kissed me.

An hour later, I dumped the bacon remnants into the trash and we carried our coffee mugs over to *Dockside* for a late breakfast. She explained that she had to leave by early afternoon, so she could make it to work on time tomorrow. After breakfast, I walked her to her car and invited her to come down again sometime, knowing that it was unlikely, but also not really caring that much.

When I got back to the boat, Dan was there, sitting on my gear box. He was dressed in a traditional white taekwondo uniform, with a black belt tied around it. "Feel up to a little work out, Jesse?" He raised both hands, palms out. "No contact, no kill."

"Yeah, sure," I replied. "Come aboard while I change."

In the salon I told him to grab a couple of water bottles from the fridge and we could go down by the boat ramp in a grassy area to spar. In my stateroom, I dug a seabag out of the bottom of the hanging closet and started hunting through the bottom of it. I found a pair of jungle camouflage utility trousers, a tan tee-shirt with a Force Recon logo on the left breast, and my black web belt. In the back of the hanging closet was a well-worn pair of black jungle boots. I pulled on the trousers, bloused them at the bottom and tucked in the tee-shirt.

When I stepped up into the salon, Dan laughed. "Is that how you dress to work out?"

I grinned at him. "This is the traditional sparring uniform of *my* people, funny guy."

We walked down the dirt road toward the boat launch and a grassy area with a couple of picnic tables off to the side. Several people from other boats and a few from *Dockside* saw us and followed. We squared off on opposite sides of the small grassy area and went through our own stretching exercises. I watched him closely as he stretched. Taekwondo, literally translated, means 'the way of the foot and the hand'. I'd studied it as a teenager, achieving brown belt status and expanded on what I'd learned in Marine Corps LINE training.

Dan did a lot of leg and back stretches. He was a kicker. LINE training has but one goal. To kill your opponent, using various kicks, hand strikes and holds from many different forms of martial arts, including Taekwondo.

My favorites were Brazilian Jiu-Jitsu and the Israeli combat fighting technique known as Krav Maga, which, in itself, is a combination of many disciplines and known to be extremely efficient and brutal.

While watching Dan, I did various stretches to loosen many muscle groups at once, never giving away any secrets as to what my style or method might be.

When we were both ready, we met in the center of the small field and bowed to one another. By now, a good dozen people had gathered around, mostly sitting on the picnic tables.

Dan was loose and quick on his feet. I assumed a modified boxers pose, crouched slightly lower. He started with a series of two quick whip kicks with his right leg, aimed at my head, which brought a cheer from the onlookers. I easily blocked the first and deflected the second. He followed that by spinning to his left with a backhanded fist strike, which I expected and ducked under. As his fist flew over my head, I spun quickly on the ball of my left foot and left hand, snaking my right leg out and catching him, not too hard, on the back of his planted right knee. It was hard enough though. His knee crumpled and as he stumbled forward, I rolled in front of him, swinging my legs up to scissor his head and snapped to my right, bringing him rolling to the ground on his back. I did a quick snap kick with my right heel, stopping it only a fraction of an inch from his throat, before rolling out and jumping to my feet.

He was up a second later. "You move a lot faster than I would have expected of a guy your size. What was that take down?"

"A form of Krav Maga, Israeli contact combat fighting."

We continued sparring for another ten minutes, each of us picking up a little more on the other's techniques and each landing focus kicks and punches that, had they connected, would have been knock out blows. He was good, better than I thought. When we finished, the crowd cheered us both as we bowed again then turned and bowed to the crowd, very theatrically.

"Your style's a little more than taekwondo," I said, as we walked back up the dirt road, both sweating and breathing hard in the crisp morning air. "I sensed a little Muay Thai there at the end, it seemed like."

He glanced over at me, as we walked. "But you caught it and countered very effectively. How many disciplines do they teach in that LINE training?"

"It varies between instructors, but the basics combine the best incapacitating techniques from boxing, Judo, Okinawan Karate, Taekwondo, Kung Fu, and Jiu-Jitsu, to name a few. I worked with the IDF, the Israeli Defense Force, for a few months in '95 and picked up some of their Krav Maga techniques."

"Can you teach me some?"

"In two weeks? Not a lot, when will you be back?"

"Early spring," he replied. "It gets too cold here in winter."

"Says the guy from Alaska." We laughed as we approached the docks. "You live aboard?" I asked.

"Yeah, down past *Dockside*, the blue and white, gaff rigged, hundred year old Friendship."

"You live on a hundred-year-old boat? That's incredible."

Dan chuckled. "Incredible maintenance." He turned to walk on down the dock. "Drop by for a beer later."

I did. After grabbing a shower and changing to my normal cargo shorts and tee-shirt I wandered up the docks past *Dockside*. His old boat was really beautiful. All wood hull with a massive wooden mast, boom, spar, and bowsprit. The mast was stepped further forward than most sloops. Dan explained that with the triple-headsail rig, the mainsail and topsail up, she carried a lot more sail area than most thirty-one footers.

"They were originally built for lobstering," he explained. "In cold weather, the cabin and bunks made for a lot more comfortable ride than the typical open boats of the time. With all that sail area, it could still be single handed easily, even while pulling lobster pots. That allowed the crew to take turns and stay warm."

The cabin was small, but beautifully appointed and very functional. A galley amidships and a convertible V-berth/settee forward in the main cabin. A quarter berth aft to starboard, under the cockpit and a small head aft to port.

The headroom was surprising. At six-three, I barely had to bend my head. Dan used the quarter berth for sleeping and had a small, folding, V-shaped table, attached to the mast that provided cozy seating for two people, forward of the galley.

We had a couple of beers in the cockpit, talking about his upcoming trip. He planned to sail, single handed, over eleven-hundred miles, from the Keys to Jost Van Dyke, in the British Virgin Islands.

"I plan to lay over in Mars Bay, on Andros then Pitt's Town, on Crooked Island, and Cockburn Town, on Grand Turk. After that, it's five or six days of open ocean to Jost Van Dyke. Two weeks to get there, altogether."

"Will you be staying in the BVI the whole time you're gone?"

"No, that's just the first gig. I'll be playing there for three weeks. After that I have another three week gig down on Anguilla, followed by more all the way down the Antilles to Dominica. Trip of a lifetime."

We talked and drank the afternoon away then it was time for him to get ready for work. He was playing the next ten days at Porky's Bayside, just before the Seven Mile Bridge.

We managed to get in a few more workouts, before his departure and soon became good friends. The day he was scheduled to leave was a Saturday late in November. It dawned overcast and gloomy, but that didn't stop all his friends from coming down to the dock to see him off. There must have been a hundred people there. The boat was well provisioned, being a former lobster boat, it could carry a lot of weight and still sail with ease. At zero-nine-hundred, Dan started his little Yanmar diesel, cast off the lines, and headed out of the harbor.

CHAPTER FIFTEEN

With the coming of December, I became more and more cranky, spending lots of time up on my island away from people. It happened every year, when I thought back on Christmases in the past. When I was little, it was a big deal around our house and my parents always made sure I received a lot of gifts. Dad was killed in Vietnam just six weeks after Christmas during the Tet Offensive, in sixty-eight. I was almost eight years old. My mom couldn't cope with it and committed suicide a few months later. I went to live with my grandparents, my dad's parents, but Christmas was never the same. Until I had kids of my own.

My two daughters live with their mom, up in Virginia now. We divorced in 1990, when I was deployed yet again. I hadn't seen my daughters in eight years and around this time of year, I missed them terribly. My ex filled their heads with lies about me and none of them wanted anything to do with me. Maybe one day I could see them again and maybe prove to them I wasn't some kind of mindless killer, like their mom told them.

Christmas came and went, as did winter. Winters in the Keys aren't as bad as Dan made out. Some days the high would only be in the low sixties, even dipping into the fifties once or twice, with lows in the forties at night. Usually, it was warm during the day and only dropped a few degrees at night.

By spring, the tourists started to thin out and the real fishermen were coming down. We kept very busy, but I still limited it to only three charters a week.

Jimmy didn't have a problem with that. He and Angie bought a houseboat and lived three slips down from me. His commute to work was about thirty steps. Our typical work day consisted of very little in the way of actual work. We sat on the bridge, drinking coffee or beer, sometimes pulling charts out and Jimmy showing me obstacles that weren't marked, or good dive spots for lobster.

As the ocean warmed, we started doing more dive charters and less fishing. Our reputation as the dive boat to charter for underwater photographers grew and by May, the end of my second year as a charter Captain, we were booked with photographers all the way through the start of lobster season. Jimmy and I agreed to not book any charters for Sportsman Weekend, the two day lobster season for sport divers. The waters were extremely over-crowded.

Earl Hailey seemed to have disappeared from the face of the earth. A lot of people thought he was nothing more than gator droppings in the mud of the Everglades, by now. The authorities came up completely empty during their month long search right after the wreck. Helicopters flew over the 'Glades daily, check points were set up on US-1 and Card Sound Road, coming into the Keys, as well as every major road leading out of the 'Glades. After a month, they gave up, coming to the same conclusion as everyone else. Earl died in the swamp.

The last Saturday in May found me at the *Anchor*, where Rusty and Julie were discussing throwing a party to celebrate the anniversary of my second year in the Keys. He wanted to make it a theme party. The theme being the Shellback ritual that Sailors and Marines have had to endure for centuries when crossing the equator aboard a warship.

"Rusty, I did that almost twenty years ago. There's no chance of me voluntarily going through that again."

"Aw, come on, Uncle Jesse," Julie said. "It sounds like it'd be a lot of fun." I'd given up trying to get her to drop the uncle bit. "Besides, you'd look good in a dress." She said the last while trying to suppress a laugh.

"Did your dad describe the initiation?" I asked her, then I turned to Rusty. "I know that even though he's a slimy Wog, he's heard about it."

"That hurts, bro," Rusty said with mocked indignation. "I was supposed to sail with you that month. It wasn't my fault I broke my leg in a HALO jump."

"A party, huh? Sure, not that we ever need an excuse around here to party. But, nothing even resembling a line crossing."

So the theme for the party was simply a party and it was scheduled for the following Saturday. Dan had arrived back in town two weeks earlier, tanned and happy, and agreed to play two sets for free beer.

The day of the party I woke early and as usual, took a thermos up to the bridge to watch the sunrise. Aaron was watering plants outside the back of the bar and walked over when he saw me.

He waved as he approached the rail. "Morning, Jesse."

"Hey Aaron, grab a mug from the galley and come on up."

"Thanks, I will." He disappeared into the salon and climbed up a moment later.

After pouring from the thermos, I said, "You're up and about early. Sun's not even up yet."

"I was actually killing time until I saw you."

"What's up?"

"Were you able to catch the news last night, or this morning?"

"I hardly ever watch TV, Aaron."

"Earl Hailey was spotted yesterday."

That got my attention. "Oh yeah? Where?"

"Robbed a liquor store up in Fort Myers. That's where you're from isn't it?"

Fort Myers? Could he be looking for me there? "Yeah," I replied. "Originally, anyway. Haven't lived there for more than twenty years."

"That's what I thought. But, I remember watching the news from the trial and when they put your picture on the screen, it said you were from Fort Myers."

"My driver's license! Damn, I've been meaning to get it renewed with my address here for two years now."

"If you haven't lived there for twenty years, why does your license have that address?"

"I kept my Florida license while I was in the Corps and used my grandparents address."

"You think he's in Fort Myers looking for you? You were the Prosecution's star witness."

I considered that. His last words to me, when Rusty and I stranded him and his buddies was 'One of these days. When you least expect it.'

"I need to make a phone call," I said, as I started down the ladder.

"Here," Aaron said. "Use my cell phone."

I stopped and sat back down. Taking his phone, I said, "Maybe I should get one of these." I dialed Directory Assistance and got the non-emergency number for the Lee County Sheriff's Office. When the duty officer answered, I gave him the address and asked if there'd been any report there of any kind of disturbance.

He put me on hold and after a minute another voice came on, "This is Detective Peter Dietrich, who is this?"

"Hi Detective. My name's Jesse McDermitt. I gave an address to…"

"Yes, Mister McDermitt, he gave me the information. What do you know about the incident?"

"That's why I'm calling, Detective. What happened at that address?"

"What's your interest?"

"I used to live there," I replied. "The house once belonged to my grandparents."

"There hasn't been any release to the media. How do you know something happened there?"

"I don't," I said, starting to get angry.

"Are you currently living in Lee County? Can you come in and talk to me?"

"No," I replied. "I live in Marathon. What happened there?"

"I really need you to drive up here, Mister McDermitt."

"I can be there in less than four hours," I said finally, knowing I wasn't going to get anywhere over the phone.

"Less than four hours? That's a good two-hundred and fifty miles."

"You know where Marina Towers is on Edisto Boulevard?"

"I know it, yeah."

"Can you pick me up there? I don't trust my truck to get to the corner store."

"How will I know you?" he asked.

"I'll tie up at the fuel dock in a forty-five foot Rampage named *Gaspar's Revenge*. A Marine flag will be flying from the bridge."

"About eleven o'clock then?"

I glanced at my watch and saw that it was only zero-six-thirty. "Maybe a little before then. I'll see you there." I closed the phone without waiting for a response and handed it back to Aaron. "Do me a favor?"

"Sure," Aaron replied. "What's going on?"

"I don't know yet. The Detective I was talking to thinks I might know something about something that happened at the house I used to live at, but wouldn't say what it was. I'm going up to meet him. Would you knock on Jimmy and Angie's hatch and let him know I'm leaving in five minutes and could use some company?"

He thanked me for the coffee and as he climbed down, I started up the big diesels. It only took me a couple of minutes to get the lines untied and was just stepping aboard when Jimmy came trotting down the dock. By the time he got aboard, I was on the bridge. I put the engines in gear and was pulling away from the dock by the time he climbed up to the bridge.

"What's going on, Skipper?"

"We're going up to Bonita Springs. Something happened up there that might have something to do with Earl Hailey and a Detective up there wants to talk to me."

We idled slowly toward the old Highway 931 Bridge, passing between the two piers that were left of it and on out into open water. I brought the *Revenge* up on plane, heading west-southwest toward the markers for Moser Channel. A few minutes later, I turned north around Pigeon Key Banks and went under the high arch of the Seven Mile Bridge. Once clear of the bridge, I made a heading of three-hundred and twenty degrees and pulled up Big Carlos Pass on the GPS. That's the entrance to Estero Bay, where Marina Towers was located. Once I engaged the auto-pilot, I pushed

the throttles on up to forty knots. That would put us there in three and a half hours.

"Mas café, por favor," I said.

"Hey!" Jimmy exclaimed. "You're picking up the lingo, man. That's good."

"Just the essentials so far. I can also order una cerveza, but it's too early for that."

"It's a start," he said. "Be back in a sec."

He took my thermos and climbed down the ladder. I switched on the intercom and said, "Grab some fruit too, I haven't had breakfast yet." He came back up a few minutes later, with a huge bowl full of sliced mango, apples, grapes, and oranges.

I kept our speed at forty knots all the way to Carlos Pass and arrived there at eleven-thirty. Dropping down off plane, but still maintaining good headway through the pass, I idled toward the high span of the bridge. The charts showed it to be twenty-three feet and the *Revenge* was only thirteen feet. Once clear of the bridge, I swung wide around the shallows and approached Marina Tower from the northeast.

The Dockmaster helped us tie off and I told him we'd be filling up and would be there hopefully for less than an hour, while I met with someone.

"It's a slow day," he said. "Once we get her filled, you can tie up just ahead there. No problem."

The unmarked cruiser pulled into the parking lot on the south side of the towers just about the time the Dockmaster finished pumping the fuel. The Detective got out of the dark blue Ford sedan and seeing my boat, started walking toward the dock, looking around. Head on a swivel.

"You must be Detective Dietrich," I said, when he was close enough to hear.

"Gunny McDermitt?"

"Ah, you did a little background," I replied.

"Served with Two-Four many years ago," he said. "Can we talk inside your boat?"

"Sure, come aboard." Turning to Jimmy I handed him several hundred dollar bills and said, "Pay the Dockmaster, Jimmy. Then see if you can scare us up a couple of burgers."

He took the hint, knowing there was plenty of food on board and sauntered off toward the marina office.

Dietrich and I went into the salon, where he whistled. "Not quite what I expected on a fishing boat."

"Want some coffee?"

"Sure."

As I was pouring he said, "I found where you once lived in the house you were asking about. I also found that you were the primary witness in the case against one Earl Hailey, who among other things is now wanted in connection with a liquor store robbery two days ago, here in Fort Myers."

I handed him the mug. "What happened at the house?"

"It hasn't been released to the press, so this is confidential. I did a little more digging and found that you're very aware of what that means, Gunny." He sat down at the settee and continued. "An elderly couple lived in the house you grew up in. William and Jane

Snodgrass. Three days ago, there was a home invasion. They were both brutally murdered."

I sat down heavily on the other side of the settee, cupping my coffee mug in both hands and staring into it. "Will and Jane were close friends of my grandparents," I finally growled. "I sold them the house after Pap died. They'd always admired it."

"Yes, I know that now. My condolences. Based on the fact that you once lived there and your driver's license and other documents still list that as your primary residence, it's an easy conclusion that Hailey went there expecting to find you. To get even."

"And people say you Detectives aren't very perceptive."

"Look, Gunny. Let the Police handle this. We'll find Hailey. We don't need you getting in the way. You understand?"

"Every cop in south Florida was looking for him a few months ago and couldn't find him. And that was after he killed one of your own."

He winced slightly at that. "We have some leads. We're going to catch him."

"How can I help?" I asked.

Dietrich asked me to go over the whole scenario, from the bar fight to the swamp, the day before the hurricane.

While I described the events, he stopped me and asked pointed questions, digging deeper into what kind of man I thought Earl to be. He kept notes with a pencil, in one of those flip notepads, just like the TV cops.

When I finished, he asked, "Why did you take this very expensive looking boat up into the Everglades before a hurricane?"

"Safest place to be," I replied. "Far enough inland to dissipate the force of the storm and it's sheltered from wind and waves."

"I don't know much about boats," he confessed. "You said you live in Boot Key Harbor now. Wouldn't a harbor protect you?"

"Boot Key is only three or four feet above sea level at the highest point. A storm surge would cover it and the harbor would become part of the Atlantic."

"I see," he said. "So, being a knowledgeable boat captain, you went up the Shark River to Tarpon Bay."

"Actually, it was a friend's advice. I've only been a skipper for two years. His family has lived in the Keys for five generations. He and his dad were caught in a sudden tropical storm once and they sheltered there when he was a kid."

"Not a lot of people have ever even heard of Tarpon Bay," he said thinking out loud. "Did you know Hailey is originally from the bayous of southern Louisiana?"

I gave that some thought. "He's a man at home in the swamp."

"A man that could survive alone in a swamp all his life would have no trouble hiding in one."

"And return to it, when he felt threatened."

Dietrich stood up and extended his hand. "Thanks, Gunny. You've been a big help."

I stood and took his hand. "Wish I could do more."

"You can't. I hope you'll take my advice and leave this to the authorities."

"You were a Magnificent Bastard?" I asked. "When?"

"Eighty-eight to ninety-two. Weapons Company."

"And you dug into my background?"

"As much as I could, legally."

"Then you know I'm not one to follow advice very well."

CHAPTER SIXTEEN

Y ou really should take his advice and stay out of
it," Julie said after I recounted my meeting with
Dietrich from earlier in the day. When Jimmy and I
left Bonita Springs, we cruised at twenty-five knots all
the way back to Marathon. The *Revenge* runs most eco-
nomically at that speed and we arrived before dark.

"Yeah, he should," Rusty agreed. "But he won't. Not
in the man's nature."

"Look," I said. "If Earl wants to find me, he'll find
me."

"He's a dangerous man, Uncle Jesse."

Rusty laughed. "He might be, in his own circle."

"What's that supposed to mean?" Julie asked, looking from her dad to me.

"It means we're running low on Red Stripe, hon,"
Rusty said. "Why don't you run out to the cooler and
bring another case in for me, would ya?"

When she left, Rusty leaned over the bar and asked, "What're you gonna do?"

"Thought I might take a camping trip," I replied.

"A camping trip?"

"Yeah, Pap used to take me way out in the swamp for weekends, when I was a kid."

"I remember them swamps," Rusty said.

"That's right," I remembered. "You came out there with us that one time, back in what, eighty-one?"

"It was '82," he said. "Got me in a world of shit with Juliet. Woman never had any qualm about me fishing for sharks, but gators? She always thought they were the spawn of Satan himself."

That night, I sat in the salon with a notepad and pencil. I put together a list of everything I might need for a week living in the swamp. It was a long list.

I had to assume Earl had some means of getting around out there, either an airboat, canoe, or skiff. There was plenty of swamp land along both the Caloosahatchee River and the Peace River. He'd also need a vehicle stashed somewhere to move around the city. I ruled out the two rivers, not remote enough. Southeast of Fort Myers is Corkscrew Swamp, home to one of the largest bald cypress stands in the world. I hiked the boardwalks through there many times, with Pap and Mam. When it was just me and Pap though, we canoed far out into it and other swamps. Corkscrew is relatively small and a popular place for bird watchers, though.

West of the city is the vast Okaloacoochee Slough State Forest land. The slough itself is over twenty square miles, surrounded by a dense cypress forest covering hundreds of square miles. While there are crushed shell roads and a few hiking trails, most of it is accessible only by canoe or kayak. I added a small canoe to my shopping list. If I were on the run, had no fear of deep, dark swampy areas, and wanted to be near Fort Myers, my choice of hiding places would be the recesses of the cypress forest surrounding Okalo-acoochee Slough.

Ground transportation was easy. I had a longtime friend, Billy Rainwater, a year behind me in high school and who I later served with, that now lived and worked in the small town of LaBelle, east of Fort My-ers. Billy was a Seminole Indian and his passion was off-roading. He owned several powerful four wheel drive pickups and had taken me off-roading a num-ber of times, whenever I was home on leave.

I found his number and made a quick phone call. He still had some off-roaders and after I explained my need to be inconspicuous, he offered me the use of an eighty-five plain Jane, white Ford Bronco, no ques-tions asked.

The next day, I fired up the old International and for once, it was amenable to the task at hand. By noon, I'd completed my shopping and had everything stored aboard the *Revenge*. Jimmy saw me moving the four-teen foot canoe to the foredeck and came over as I was lashing it down.

"What's with the canoe, man?" he asked.

"We need to reschedule the charters for about a week," I said by way of reply.

"A week?" he asked. "That's gonna be some pissed off picture takers, man."

"I have to go somewhere," I said

"You're going after that Earl dude, aren't you?"

"Just keep that to yourself, Jimmy."

"Sure, man. When are we leaving?"

"I'm leaving in an hour. You're staying here." I could see by his expression it hurt him. "I'm going way back in the swamps and it could be dangerous."

"You're the boss, man. Hey, I could help ya get across, then just stay on the boat, while you go play Tarzan."

"Could be dangerous on the boat, too. I know you can look out for yourself, but I'd still be worried."

That seemed to satisfy him. "I'll take care of re-scheduling the clients. You'll be gone a whole week?"

"Hopefully less. But, if I can't track him down in a week, I'll give up," I lied. The truth was, I was going to find Hailey, no matter how long it took.

"Vaya con Dios, Jeffe," he said as he started to walk away.

"Gracias, mi amigo. Voy a regresar muy pronto," I said back with a grin.

"Aw, now you're just showing off," he called back over his shoulder as he walked back to the houseboat.

Forty minutes later, I had everything aboard and stowed away. I started the engines and climbed down to untie the lines. A few minutes later I was idling away from the docks and heading toward the bridge. Once I cleared the inlet to the harbor, I brought the boat up on plane. Dark clouds were building to the east, but they seemed to be moving away.

Keeping at cruising speed, I got to San Carlos Bay in five hours and started up the Caloosahatchee River to LaBelle. Once past the I-75 bridge, the river narrowed and I had to drop down off plane. I still had another twenty-five miles to Port Labelle Marina, where I'd made arrangements to dock the *Revenge*. Arriving just after sunset, I called the Dockmaster on channel sixteen and requested directions to the fuel dock.

After fueling up, he assigned me a slip with shore power, water, cable TV, and a phone line. Once I was tied up and connected, I called Billy and told him where I was staying for the night. He said it was only a few blocks away and he'd drive the truck over with a cooler full of beer and some steaks and then he could walk home.

When I saw him pull into the parking lot, I flashed the cockpit lights on and off. He parked the truck and walked down the dock carrying a cooler in one hand and a plastic bag in the other. He was wearing blue jeans, a white tee-shirt, a cowboy hat, and his feet were bare. Nearly as tall as me, he looked to have put on weight, which was good. He'd always been a gangly, thin man.

"Good to see you, Billy," I called out.

"Same here, Kemosabe. Been what, ten years?"

I took the cooler he handed me and placed it on the deck. "Nine, I think. Just before I left for Beirut. How've you been?"

He leaped over the gunwale and took my forearm in his hand, shaking hands Indian style. "Making my way in the white man's world as best I can, Jesse. You look fit. I thought you said you were retired?"

"Yeah, two years ago. What's being fit got to do with retired?"

"Nothing. But, you're still wearing that high and tight. Let your hair grow, man."

I laughed. "Some habits die a little harder than others. Come on inside."

I opened the hatch and we stepped up into the salon. Billy was never one to be impressed by much of anything material and I didn't expect any reaction. "Where you want me to put these steaks?" he asked.

"Just set 'em on the counter there. I just put some potatoes in the oven, we can grill the steaks out in the cockpit in a bit."

He set them down and turned around, a serious look on his face. "What kinda man are you hunting and where?"

"Who said I was hunting someone?"

"You got a canoe strapped to your foredeck, you want to borrow an inconspicuous truck, there's a box of seven-point-six-twos in that partially open drawer, and well, you're you."

"Have a seat," I said, matching his tone. "You hear about a liquor store robbery a couple days ago, over in Fort Myers?"

"I knew it! The news said he was an escaped convict, recapped his trial and your face popped up on the screen."

"What the news didn't say was that he broke into the house I used to live in."

"The one you sold to the Snodgrasses?"

"They're dead," I said flatly.

Billy plopped down on the cushion of the settee, like he'd been poleaxed. Will and Jane were very close friends with his parents. Probably the only white people way back in the day that were.

"Dead? I just saw Mister Snodgrass last week. He visited dad in the home, while I was there."

"How is your dad?"

He seemed to shake his whole body and sigh. "About the same. He stares out the window all day and never says anything."

Billy's dad, William 'Leaping Panther' Rainwater, was a Chieftain among his people, one of the few Calusa Indians left in the area. They once covered most of southwest Florida until the Spaniards arrived with their diseases. In the fifties, the Calusa were forced onto the Seminole reservation, where Leaping Panther met Billy's mother, a Seminole. They were in a car wreck about twelve years ago, his mother was killed and his father was in a coma for weeks. When he came out of it and Billy told him his wife of thirty years was dead, he never spoke again. Although alert to what happened around him, he seemed to choose to ignore it.

Billy's thumbnail scraped at the label on his beer bottle. After a moment, he looked up, his dark eyes smoldering. "I'm going with you," he whispered.

"I can't ask you to do that."

"You don't have to. The Snodgrasses were like family. Besides your people, they were the only whites that didn't see color."

I considered it a moment. Will and Jane never had children and treated myself and Billy like their own. He was right, we were family.

I nodded. "Okay, we leave at first light."

While we drank beer and cooked the steaks on a grill mounted to a pole that fit into a rod holder, I explained what I knew about Hailey and where I thought he might be hiding out.

"That's over two hundred square miles," he said when I finished. "Most of it inaccessible to any kind of vehicle, except canoes or kayaks. Airboats ain't allowed in there."

"They'd be too noisy for him anyway," I said. "I brought something along that might make it a little easier."

I went up into the salon and came back out a moment later with the night vision headsets Rusty and I used to ambush Earl and his crew on Shark River.

Handing one to Billy, I said, "At night, he's got to have a fire, probably very small, just to cook on and keep the bugs at bay. With these, we can see that fire from half a mile away. I also have a pair of handheld VHF radios."

We ate the steaks and then climbed up on the bridge with a couple more beers. We talked about old times for a while then Billy said he had a couple things he'd need to get from his house and gave me directions to it, preferring to walk home. We agreed that I'd pick him up at zero-six-hundred and we'd head out to Oka-loacoochee Slough from there. After he left, I took advantage of the darkness and loaded the Bronco with everything I'd brought.

CHAPTER SEVENTEEN

I woke at zero-five-thirty and filled my thermos with coffee. After I secured the *Revenge* and set the alarm I got in the Bronco and drove the three blocks to Billy's house. He was waiting on the porch and rose as I pulled up. He walked down the sidewalk, carrying a Remington 700 rifle. The 700 is the platform that the M40 is built on. Chambered for .308 ammunition, it's a very accurate rifle, favored by deer hunters.

When he opened the back door I said, "There's an empty fly rod case that'll fit into on the back seat."

Without a word, he opened the case and put the rifle in it. I figured he'd be bringing his dad's old rifle. I helped him lift his wooden canoe up onto the roof and strap it down next to mine. Then we got in the truck and started driving. We were both quiet. No words needed to be spoken. We didn't have very far to go.

Growing up in Lee and Hendry Counties, both of us loved the outdoors. We fished and hunted together as

soon as we were old enough. Billy was a great, natural tracker and could follow a feral hog or deer for miles through the dense forest. But, today we were hunting the most dangerous animal in the forest. Man.

Thirteen miles due south of LaBelle, Highway 29 ran as straight as the proverbial arrow, like many roads in Florida. There just weren't any obstacles to road building in the early days, besides swamp and trees, which were pretty much everywhere. The early road builders laid out grids and built roads in straight lines.

I turned off onto Keri Road, which goes through the State Forest from the west, to the park office. We had no intention of registering to camp, though. After four miles on the paved road, I turned south onto Sic Island Road, which is really just two overgrown ruts, that wound its way south, deeper into the cypress forest.

As we bounced over the rough terrain, there were occasional glimpses of pasture land to the west, but everything to the east was shrouded in dark shadows from the dense cypress trees, the ground soft and spongy. After a half mile the road ended at the trailhead of Sic Island Loop. Billy, myself, and many of our friends had hiked the trails through the forest many times and as teenagers, we'd brought our dates to this very spot, deep in the forest. Although it had been many years since I was last here, nothing had changed. The swamps, like the stars above, are timeless. We knew that on a weekday morning, there wouldn't be anyone around to see us unpack and there wasn't.

I'd chosen this spot well in advance, as it's not a popular hiking area, most hikers preferred the manicured trails on the east side of the slough, near the park office. Here, in the center of the west side of the park we had all of Okaloacoochee Slough State Forest to the east of us.

Without need of direction, we both climbed from the truck and unloaded the two canoes. Within ten minutes we had everything unpacked from the truck and pushed off into the dark, tannin water. I let Billy lead the way.

We paddled south, rounded Sic Island and made our way to the southern tip of the island. Being the beginning of the rainy season, the water was low and we had to get out and portage a very shallow spit to deeper water.

Once across, we paddled south, our goal being a small island just south of Sic Island on the western fringe of the forest. The whole forest is covered with small lakes and ponds, all joined together in the rainy season. In dry season, like now, you had to know your way through the endless tangle of shallow and deeper waters unless you didn't mind getting out and dragging your canoe across the shallows.

We were completely enveloped in the shadowy, primordial swamp, paddling slowly and quietly between towering bald cypress trees that created a nearly impenetrable canopy above.

The slough was home to thousands of alligators and we saw quite a few, hauled up on logs, or shallow flats. It was also home to black bears and Florida panthers, a distant cousin of the cougar. Few people ever left the well-marked trails as we were doing, for just the same reason that made me think this was where we'd find Hailey. It was remote and wild.

After another hour of paddling, we set up camp. Tents were too dangerous out here. We strung hammocks high up in the cypress trees, with netting that would keep the mosquitoes out. We ate a cold lunch of MRE's, meals-ready-to-eat.

"We'll head out just after sunset," I told Billy. "It'd be a waste of time to search in daylight."

"How certain are you that this man killed the Snodgrasses?"

"His last words to me, when I stranded him up Shark River were, 'One of these days. When you least expect it.' An obvious threat. I was told that during the trial, the news talked about me being a witness, showed a picture of me and said I was from Fort Myers. I haven't renewed my license since Pap died and it still has my old address on it. Wouldn't take a rocket scientist to figure out where to look for me."

"So he went there to settle the score and the Snodgrasses just got in the way?"

"That's the way I figure it. He used to live way back in the bayou up in Louisiana. A man like that would be at home out here. Plenty of game to trap, no prying eyes, and easy to come and go."

"Why not the swamps along the Peace or Caloosahatchee?"

"Not much left," I said. "People canoe both rivers, lots of boat traffic on the Caloosahatchee, and it's a short distance to civilization, just steps from the river."

"And Big Cypress is too far away from Fort Myers, where he thinks you are."

"That leaves Okaloacoochee, or Corkscrew," I said.

"Humph, Corkscrew ain't much these days. Most of the land's been drained and planted."

"Which puts us right here," I said.

"You say this man killed a prison guard and another convict to get away?" he asked.

I knew what Billy was trying to do. He was trying to justify, in his own mind, what we were about to do. He suspected that I hadn't come out here to capture Earl Hailey.

"Yeah," I said. "That was after he'd been convicted of attempting to murder a man out pleasure cruising with his family, then kidnapping and raping his wife and their two daughters, over a three week period, with three of his friends. And those were just the ones they could prove. I'd bet there were others, before that. He was planning to sell the mother and girls in the sex slave market. The daughters were thirteen and fifteen."

I knew that would help ease his mind on what we were going to do. Billy had three daughters and a son, all in their early teens and pre-teens. I watched as I saw the steely resolve transform his dark eyes into smoldering embers. Billy was a basic infantryman back in the day and had served in Grenada with the Twenty-Second Amphibs. Though he never talked about it,

I knew he was not a stranger to the taking of a man's life.

"We should get some rest," he finally said.

We climbed up into the trees and got comfortable in our hammocks. It wasn't very hot and there was a light breeze blowing. I'd never had trouble sleeping during the day. I'd learned over the years to get rest anytime and anywhere possible.

The alarm on my watch woke me a few hours later. The sun was just slipping below the invisible horizon and it was already quite dark under the cypress canopy. I could hear Billy stirring in his hammock.

I climbed down, and by the last paltry light filtering through the trees, I made my way over to the canoes. I barely heard Billy as he dropped from the tree and didn't hear his footsteps at all. Then he was suddenly standing right beside me, as though he was some kind of silent apparition. I opened a watertight box in my canoe and took out five MRE's, handing four to Billy.

"Stow all but one for later," I whispered. "If we don't find him before dawn, we'll meet back here."

We sat on the bows of the two canoes, eating the cold food. We'd already decided that while we were out here, we'd run a cold camp. No fire. It got dark really fast and within minutes I couldn't see my hand in front of my face.

I felt around in the canoe and opened another watertight box and handed Billy one of the night vision headsets and a VHF radio. We donned the headsets and switched them on. Looking around, I could see everything clearly, though with a grainy, grayish-green tint. We opened the fly rod cases and inspected and loaded the weapons. Outside of the M40 having a fiberglass stock and Billy's Remington having a wood stock, they were identical.

"I brought backup sidearms, if you want one," I said.

"Got my own," he replied, opening a case and removing an old 1911 Colt .45 semiautomatic and thrust it in the back of his jeans. "What do we do if and when we find this man?"

Billy was still having some misgivings. "If you find him, call me on the radio and I'll do the same. We'll rendezvous and give him a chance to give up."

"And if he doesn't?"

"I'll kill him and feed him to the gators."

"Just like that?"

"Yeah, Billy. Just like that."

He looked out over the swamp for a moment and then turned toward me and with no consternation said, "Okay."

We shoved off, going in opposite directions. The state forest land covered almost thirty-five-thousand acres, but the wetland part on the west, the densest and least accessible part, was only a couple miles wide and six miles long. It was still a huge area to cover in canoes.

I went south, paddling slowly through the dense forest. Both of us had explored these wetlands by canoe and kayak hundreds of times, so there was little chance of either of us getting lost. What I was hoping for was that Earl would be holed up on one of the hundreds of tiny islands and would have a small fire going. A fire, that with the aid of the night vision goggles, would be visible for quite a distance.

After more than three miles of paddling, I reached the southern part of the wetlands, where it narrowed and flowed into Big Cypress Swamp and Fakahatchee Strand. I was outside the state park boundaries and in Collier County now.

I picked up the small VHF and keyed the mic. "Billy," I whispered. I heard only a click in return.

"At the south end," I said. "I'm turning and going up the east side now."

"Past Sears. I'm north of Oil Well Pad, heading south," came his whispered reply, meaning he'd reached the northernmost part of the wetlands, where the abandoned sawmill town of Sears was located and had crossed over to the east side where an old oil well head was located. He'd covered a lot more distance than I had, but I figured he would.

An hour after I started heading north, the radio clicked once. I picked it up and listened for a moment but there was only silence. I keyed the mic. "Billy?"

He replied in a faint whisper, "I see light."

"Where?" I whispered back.

"South end of Butterfly," he whispered, meaning Butterfly Island, right in the center of the forest. I'd passed the western side of it going south and should have seen it.

"Meet me on the west side of Patterson Hammock," I said and then put the radio down and started paddling. I was a mile away.

When I got to within a half mile of Butterfly Island, I could see light filtering through the trees ahead. I struck out to the northeast, where I figured Billy would already be waiting. Twenty minutes later, the radio clicked again.

I stopped paddling and whispered, "Go."

Billy whispered back, "You whites make too much noise. Look to your one o'clock."

Ahead about a hundred yards and just off to the right, I could see Billy sitting in his canoe. I paddled toward him as quietly as I could. Once alongside, he whispered, "He's not alone."

"How many?

"Just him and a young woman. I don't think she's there by choice. Don't look directly at the fire. Lean over here and look to the right of the light and wait for the optics to adjust."

I leaned over his canoe, which put a cypress tree between me and the fire, blocking most of the light. The campsite came into sharp focus after a few seconds. It was Earl, alright. I checked my watch, it was almost zero-one-hundred. Looking back at his camp, I saw the woman. I couldn't see much of her as she had her back to me, doing something over the fire. Earl was sitting on a log a few feet away. There was a small tent behind him. While he might know the Louisiana bayous, it didn't seem he was aware of the concentration of panthers in this area.

"How do you want to play this?" Billy asked.

I thought it over for a moment. For Billy's sake, I wanted to give the man at least half a chance. If it were just me, I'd put the cross hairs on his forehead and pull the trigger from here.

"What made you say she wasn't out here by choice?"

"Look closer," he said. "She has a chain around her left ankle."

I watched, but still couldn't see a chain. Then she stood up and carried what looked like a pan over toward Earl. She held the pan in one hand and a length of chain in the other that hung down and was shackled to her ankle.

"Another captive," I whispered. "Damn."

"So, how you want to do this, Kemosabe?"

I thought about it again. "See that deadfall, just ahead of us. You paddle up there and use it to steady that Remington. I'm going to paddle over to the far side and come up behind him. I'll turn on the infrared light on my headset and you'll be able to see me clearly, but he won't. I have a set of headphones for this radio and you can keep me informed of anything. When I'm close enough to see by the firelight, I'll ditch the headset and wait a few minutes to let my eyes adjust. Then I'll just walk into his camp, with my Sig and you can cover me."

"Guess that works as well as anything. Way out here, on a weeknight, he won't be expecting anyone."

"It'll take me a good thirty minutes to get around there," I said as I pushed away from his canoe. I paddled in what I hoped was total silence and made it to the far side of Butterfly Island in twenty minutes.

I switched on the tiny infrared light on the headset. It was all but invisible more than six inches away, but illuminated my path greatly and subdued the ambient light from the fire. Through Billy's headset, it would be seen clearly as I crept quietly through the forest toward the camp. The ground was soft and spongy, but I had to go slow to avoid any dead twigs.

"Stop," Billy's voice came over the earphones. "He's looking around. Nod if you stepped on something." I froze where I was. I hadn't made the slightest sound and knew there was no way Earl could hear me.

"He looks troubled," Billy whispered. "I think the bugs might have stopped making noise. Just don't move for a second and they'll start again."

He was right, the chirping near me had stopped. Within a few seconds they started again. "Move slower," Billy whispered. "Bugs sense pressure changes, not sound."

I started moving again, ever so slowly, taking several seconds to move one leg forward and take a single step. I could hear Earl now, talking to the woman, but couldn't make out what he was saying. Slowly, I kept moving forward, keeping a large tree between me and the fire.

After what seemed like a really long time, I was close enough to hear him. "Yeah, we're gonna have us a party tonight, bitch. Just as soon as I finish eating."

I was close enough now. I switched the infrared light off and on three times then removed the headset and placed it on the ground at my feet.

"Don't rush," Billy whispered. "Give your eyes a couple of minutes to adjust. I have him covered and I can see you and her both. You're in the shadows and there's no way he can see you."

I nodded in the darkness. Slowly, my eyes adjusted to the near darkness. Only the light from the small fire illuminated the night. What had appeared to be a roaring bonfire in the night vision optics, was actually a very small fire, mostly coals and very little flame.

Earl was eating something straight out of the pan using his fingers and when he finished, just tossed the pan to the side, picked up a beer can and took a long pull.

"Get over here, bitch," he growled. "Time you earned your keep again."

I took four quick steps, coming out from the shadows, leading with my Sig. "You're gonna have to wait, Earl. If you so much as move a muscle, I'll shoot you." Earl froze. He'd been taken completely by surprise and I could tell from his expression that he was thinking about it.

"Pistol in his pants," Billy shouted, no longer bothering to use the VHF. "Left side, cross draw."

"You and I have been through this drill before, Earl. Use your left hand, real slow. Pull that pistol out and toss it on the ground. You're covered by a high powered rifle."

When Billy shouted, Earl looked toward the sound and I took two more steps into the light. "You!" he growled. "How the fuck?"

"I'm not gonna say it again, Earl. Toss that pistol now, or I'll blow your damn head off."

I could see in his eyes that he was calculating his chances. Then resignation came over his face and he moved his left hand very slowly to his side and pulled a Beretta semiautomatic from his waist band with his thumb and forefinger. Holding it up, he tossed it away.

Unfortunately for Earl, he tossed it near the woman. In a flash, she snatched it up from the ground, leveled it at Hailey, thumbed the hammer and before I could shout no, she fired. The first round spun Earl half way around where he sat. She fired again and caught him in the neck, blood spraying behind him, as he fell backward off the log. She stepped forward, firing over and over, into Earl's lifeless body. I ran toward the woman, as she continued pulling the trigger, until the slide locked to the rear.

Billy splashed through the water, coming toward us as the woman fell to her knees. She tossed the gun aside and hung her head into her hands, sobbing. I hurried over to where Earl lay on the ground, his lifeless eyes staring up at the cypress canopy.

Billy went to the woman, kneeling down and taking her in his arms, talking to her soothingly, telling her she was alright and we'd get her out safely.

I holstered my Sig and walked over to where Billy was helping the woman to her feet. "Are you gonna arrest me?" she managed to croak out between sobs.

"We're not the law," I said. "You're safe now. What's your name?"

"You're not the police?"

"No ma'am," Billy said. "Just a couple guys who heard noise and came to see what was going on."

Between sobs, she said, "I'm Regina Castillo."

Billy smiled. "That's good, Miss Castillo. Now, with your permission, I'd like to take that chain off your leg. Will that be alright with you?"

She nodded, then looked at the dead man on the ground. "He has the key."

I went over to the body, searched his pockets and found a key ring. I handed it to Billy, who seemed to have begun to build a trust with the young woman. Up close, she was older than I first thought, maybe late twenties.

Billy bent down and gently tried several keys from the key ring until he finally unsnapped the padlock that secured the chain to her ankle and stood up.

"There ya go, Miss Castillo. Is there anything here that belongs to you that you want to take with you? We're going to take you to safety now."

"Who, who are you guys?" she asked. Looking at me she said, "You called that man by name."

"I'm sorry," I said. "Billy lied. We came out here looking for that man, but we aren't the law."

"Is he.... dead?"

"Yes, ma'am," Billy said. "Are you going to be okay? Is there anything you need to bring with you?"

"No," she said. "He took everything I had. Kept my money and credit cards and threw everything else away."

"Then let's get going. Jesse, I'll take Miss Castillo in my canoe, while you tend to things here. Once we get around to where your canoe is, we can go to our camp, grab our gear and get out of here."

I nodded. "Are you sure there's nothing here that belongs to you, ma'am? Anything at all that might tie you to this place?"

That seemed to frighten her for a second, the thought that we might be more of the same. Billy put his hands on the woman's shoulders and looked into her eyes. "What Jesse means is, you were never here. You don't know anything about how that man died. Hunting accidents happen all the time." He grinned and looked at me, "Right Kemosabe?"

I nodded, "Absolutely, Tonto."

She laughed then and it sounded good. "No, there's absolutely nothing here that's mine."

"Good. You go with Billy, he'll bring you around to where my canoe is. Our camp is only a mile from here. We'll get our stuff and it's less than half a mile from there to where our truck is. We'll have you back in civilization by dawn. Where do you live?"

"Coral Springs. Where are we anyway? He put me in the trunk of my car and we drove for hours."

"This is a state park," I said. "We're just outside Fort Myers. Do you know where your car is?"

"That animal burned it," she said as we walked her through the shallow water toward Billy's canoe. "He kidnapped me while I was getting gas, um, four days ago, I think. My husband's probably worried to death."

"You can call him from my house," Billy said. "My wife's about the same size, you can borrow some clothes, get cleaned up and rest a little, before your husband gets there. Or would you prefer to go to the police?"

She stopped and looked back at Earl's camp. "No," she said to me. "If you can make this nightmare disappear, we can leave the police out of it."

"Good choice," I said. "I can do that."

I turned and went back to the camp, while they sloshed through the water to Billy's canoe. I searched Earl's pockets, but didn't find much. I pocketed three credit cards and a small wad of cash to give to the woman. I stripped his clothes off, wadded them up and tossed them on the fire. Looking inside the tent, I found a single sleeping bag and a nearly empty cooler. I took the water and beer, poured them out, crushed the cans and bottles, and tossed them in the fire. Throwing a couple more pieces of dead wood on, it began blazing. I tore down the tent, rolled it up with the sleeping bag still inside and tossed it on the fire. When it was roaring good, I up-ended the cooler and put it on the fire, before adding even more wood. Within a few hours there'd be nothing left of any of it, not even the aluminum cans.

With all the plastic and nylon, the fire was soon very hot. I went over to Earl's body and taking it by the arms, I dragged it over near the canoe and wedged it between two cypress trees, then piled some dead palm fronds around it. I picked up my night vision head set, put it on and looked out over the water. Several pairs of flickering red eyes looked back. Within an hour, the gators would take care of Earl and the panthers would carry off the rest. By dawn, there wouldn't be anything left.

Keeping my back to the fire, I walked around the camp, looking for anything else through the night vision. I picked up the chain and lock and flung them both out into the water, then returned to my canoe.

Several gators had moved in closer and one was swimming straight toward the body. Maybe it wouldn't even take until dawn.

Putting one foot in the canoe, I shoved off. Within minutes, I was a hundred feet from shore and looking off to my left, I saw Billy and the woman in his canoe heading toward me. As they pulled alongside, several splashes could be heard from shore. The gators would make short work of their grizzly task.

"What's that?" Regina asked.

"You don't want to know," Billy replied. "Let's get you out of here, Miss Castillo."

# EPILOGUE

Billy and I got Regina Castillo to his house before sunrise. After spending ten minutes on the phone with her husband and convincing him she was safe, she hung up and told us that she'd told her husband she'd been abducted but managed to get away. Billy's wife, Hanna, gave her some clean clothes and showed her to the bathroom, so she could get cleaned up.

I took Billy outside and said, "I'm going home. Tell Regina that I never existed, okay. She wandered out of the swamp and found you and Hanna sitting on the porch. Whoever snatched her, left her to die and she never saw his face."

"I'll take care of it, Jesse. Don't worry. Just leave the keys to the truck in it, nobody'll bother it."

I took his outstretched forearm in mine then leaned in and embraced my old friend. "Come down to Marathon, we'll go fishing."

"I'll do that," he said as I walked toward the truck.

By noon, I was tied up at *Dockside* again, like nothing had ever happened. Jimmy was able to rework the schedule and we managed to get all our charters in for the week. Even those that had to reschedule were happy with the outcome.

Summer wore on and before we knew it, fall had arrived again. Billy never did come down, but with a wife, four kids, a job, and his four wheeling hobby, I wasn't counting on it.

In early September, I finally got around to changing my driver's license. I was sitting in the DMV office, waiting for my number to be called, looking out at a clear blue sky. There was a commotion in one of the offices behind the counter and several of the clerks crowded around the door. I walked over to see what the commotion was about and they were watching a small TV in the office. On the screen I could see there was a news report covering a high rise fire.

I was starting to get impatient and was about to say something, when I watched on the screen as a jumbo jet flew into a different building, exploding on impact. *How could an airline pilot hit a building?* I thought. Then the camera panned out and I saw two buildings on fire. I recognized the landmark immediately. The World Trade Centers.

Later, at the *Anchor*, we watched it on the news over and over, along with footage of a burning Pentagon. Within a few days we learned that terrorists had hijacked four airliners and flown them into the Twin Towers and the Pentagon. Some gutsy passengers tried to take control of the fourth and it went down in a field in Pennsylvania.

Everyone was in shock for days, it seemed. We all stumbled around, not sure what to do or say. Saturday morning, I borrowed Rusty's pickup and drove to Miami. By zero-nine-hundred, I was sitting in a Marine Corps Recruiter's office on US-1, in Cutler Bay, just south of the city. I had my retirement papers in hand and was talking to a prior service recruiter.

"Gunny," the young Staff Sergeant said, "I wish there was something I could do, but right now HQMC is saying no prior service, that have been out for more than two years, regardless of rank. Let's leave this one to the young guns."

I left the office feeling more dejected than ever in my life. There was no doubt in my mind our country was going to war and apparently it didn't need me anymore. I felt even older than when Julie calls me 'uncle'.

When I got back home, I made a few phone calls to some high ranking Officers I used to know. A couple of them owed me. I called in every marker, to no avail. I wasn't even forty years old and I was already a washed up has-been.

I spent hours watching the news, an armchair quarterback. As winter wore on, I lost interest in doing any charter fishing at all.

The new President seemed to have everything in hand and the American military machine began to spool up for the coming conflict. By early October, President Bush's catch phrase was the 'War on Terror'.

By spring, I'd come to grips with the fact that I was an old warrior, like one of the guys that sat around the VFW and reminisced about their glory days. My friends pumped me up every chance they could and Jimmy kept coming to me with offers to charter. I finally started easing my way back into my new career and by April we were back to three charters a week.

Julie celebrated her twentieth birthday and was constantly pushing me to 'get back in the saddle', as she called it. I hadn't been on a date since before the attacks and hadn't even met a woman that interested me.

One Saturday afternoon, I was sitting on the bridge enjoying the first cold beer of the day and watching the goings on in the marina. A yellow Jeep Cherokee pulled into the parking lot, towing a nice looking blue and white flats skiff, with a big Mercury outboard hanging on the back. What caught my eye was the license tag on both the trailer and the car. Oregon tags.

I watched as the driver turned around in front of the boat ramp and started backing up. Sometimes, people do the stupidest things when launching their boats, so the boat ramp was always fun to watch. This guy backed up straight and true, without pulling up once. When the driver's door opened, I sat up straight in my chair and leaned forward.

It was a woman. Not just any woman, either. She was tall and had the broad shoulders you see on some professional swimmers and a slim waist. She had thick, wavy, blond hair past her shoulders. As she walked back to the trailer, she pulled her hair back and put one of those elastic bands around it, then pulled a long billed fishing cap out of the pocket of her cargo shorts and put it on.

I watched as she pulled a line from the front of the skiff and tied it to the front of the trailer. She released the crank, turned out a little slack and unhooked the cable from the skiff. As she walked back to the car, she looked around the marina and saw me staring at her. She smiled and waved. I stood up and waved back.

She backed the boat down the ramp, stopping at just the right moment and the little skiff slid off the trailer, floating just behind it. The safety line never even tightened up. She pulled forward slightly, so the front of the trailer was out of the water then got out again. After untying the safety line and tying it off to a cleat on the dock, she parked the car and trailer. A few minutes later, she walked down to the ramp with two fly rod cases in one hand and a tackle box in the other. Moments after that, she disappeared past the old bridge. Realizing I'd been staring the whole time, I sat back down and finished my beer.

Aaron came out the back door of his office and I whistled to get his attention then motioned him over. I climbed down and stepped up to the dock as he walked up.

"Say, Aaron. Did you see that yellow Cherokee that just launched?"

"Of course. People have to pay to use our ramp."

"I don't suppose you got her name, did you?"

He grinned. "Yeah, her name's Alexis, but she said to call her Alex. Alex DuBois. From Oregon."

"Alex DuBois," I repeated as I turned and looked toward the bridge where she'd just disappeared.

THE END

If you enjoyed reading this short novel and would like to receive a newsletter from the author for specials and updates on upcoming books, please sign up on the website:

www.waynestinnett.com

Jesse McDermitt Series
Fallen Out
Fallen Palm
Fallen Hunter
Fallen Pride
Fallen Mangrove
Fallen King
Fallen Honor
Fallen Tide (November, 2015)

Charity Styles Series
Merciless Charity
Ruthless Charity (Winter, 2016)
Heartless Charity (Fall, 2016)

The Gaspar's Revenge Ship's Store is now open. There you can purchase all kinds of swag related to my books.
WWW.GASPARS-REVENGE.COM

ABOUT THE AUTHOR

Wayne Stinnett is a Veteran of the United States Marine Corps and novelist. After serving he worked as a deckhand, commercial fisherman, Divemaster, taxi driver, construction manager, and commercial truck driver. He currently lives in the foothills of the Blue Ridge Mountains, near Travelers Rest, SC with his wife and youngest daughter. They have three other children, three grandchildren, three dogs and a whole flock of parakeets. He's the founder of the local Marine Corps League detachment in nearby Greenville and rides with the Patriot Guard Riders. He grew up in Melbourne, FL. He's also lived in Marathon, FL, in the fabulous Florida Keys, Andros Island, Bahamas, Dominica in the Windward Islands, and Cozumel, Mexico.

Wayne began writing in 1988, penning three short stories before setting it aside to deal with life as a new father. He took it up again at the urging of his third wife and youngest daughter, who love to hear his 'sea stories'. Those three short stories formed the basis of his first novel, Fallen Palm. After a year of working on it, he published it in October, 2013.

Since then, he's written more novels and now this prequel in the Jesse McDermitt Caribbean Adventure Series. The first novel in a new spin-off series will be available in the summer of 2015.

Made in the USA
Columbia, SC
24 April 2018